AROUND CHI-TOWN

Breaking news! Charlotte Masters, the missing assistant to business tycoon Grant Connelly, is allegedly the target of a hit man. After being questioned by police for her role in the illegal doings at Connelly Corporation, Charlotte dodged the first hit attempt. But why the mysterious woman declined police protection is anyone's guess. Does this reportedly "honest woman" have something to hide? And Ms. Masters may not be the only one on the run— rumor has it she's pregnant, so where's the baby's dad?

Missing son Rafe Connelly has returned to Chicago to help solve the family's troubles. The renowned computer whiz is looking into technological tampering at Connelly Corporation. But it may be too late to stem the tide at the beloved Chicago institution. With its flood of troubles, the Connellys may need more than Rafe's genius to keep them afloat.

Dear Reader,

Wondering what to put on your holiday wish list? How about six passionate, powerful and provocative new love stories from Silhouette Desire!

This month, bestselling author Barbara Boswell returns to Desire with our MAN OF THE MONTH, SD #1471, *All in the Game*, featuring a TV reality-show contestant who rekindles an off-screen romance with the chief cameraman while her identical twin wonders what's going on.

In SD #1472, *Expecting…and In Danger* by Eileen Wilks, a Connelly hero tries to protect and win the trust of a secretive, pregnant lover. It's the latest episode in the DYNASTIES: THE CONNELLYS series—the saga of a wealthy Chicago-based clan.

A desert prince loses his heart to a feisty intern in SD #1473, *Delaney's Desert Sheikh* by award-winning author Brenda Jackson. This title marks Jackson's debut as a Desire author. In SD #1474, *Taming the Prince* by Elizabeth Bevarly, a blue-collar bachelor trades his hard hat for a crown…and a wedding ring? This is the second Desire installment in the exciting CROWN AND GLORY series.

Matchmaking relatives unite an unlikely couple in SD #1475, *A Lawman in Her Stocking* by Kathie DeNosky. And SD #1476, *Do You Take This Enemy?* by reader favorite Sara Orwig, is a marriage-of-convenience story featuring a pregnant heroine whose groom is from a feuding family. This title is the first in Orwig's compelling STALLION PASS miniseries.

Make sure you get all six of Silhouette Desire's hot November romances.

Enjoy!

Joan Marlow Golan

Joan Marlow Golan
Senior Editor, Silhouette Desire

Please address questions and book requests to:
Silhouette Reader Service
U.S.: 3010 Walden Ave., P.O. Box 1325, Buffalo, NY 14269
Canadian: P.O. Box 609, Fort Erie, Ont. L2A 5X3

Expecting...
and In Danger
EILEEN WILKS

Published by Silhouette Books

America's Publisher of Contemporary Romance

Special thanks and acknowledgment are given to Eileen Wilks for her contribution to the DYNASTIES: THE CONNELLYS series.

My thanks to all the other authors who participated in this continuity—what a great bunch!—with special hugs for Leanne and Sheri. I also want to thank Patricia Rosemoor for her help with streets, neighborhoods and buildings in Chicago. Harlequin and Silhouette writers are some of the most generous people anywhere.

 SILHOUETTE BOOKS

ISBN 0-373-76472-3

EXPECTING...AND IN DANGER

Visit Silhouette at www.eHarlequin.com

Printed in U.S.A.

Books by Eileen Wilks

Silhouette Desire

The Loner and the Lady #1008
The Wrong Wife #1065
Cowboys Do It Best #1109
Just a Little Bit Pregnant #1134
Just a Little Bit Married? #1188
Proposition: Marriage #1239
The Pregnant Heiress #1378
*Jacob's Proposal #1397
*Luke's Promise #1403
*Michael's Temptation #1409
Expecting…and In Danger #1472

Silhouette Intimate Moments

The Virgin and the Outlaw #857
Midnight Cinderella #921
Midnight Promises #982
Night of No Return #1028
Her Lord Protector #1160

*Tall, Dark & Eligible

EILEEN WILKS

is a fifth-generation Texan. Her great-great-grandmother came to Texas in a covered wagon shortly after the end of the Civil War—excuse us, the War Between the States. But she's not a full-blooded Texan. Right after another war, her Texan father fell for a Yankee woman. This obviously mismatched pair proceeded to travel to nine cities in three countries in the first twenty years of their marriage, raising two kids and innumerable dogs and cats along the way. For the next twenty years they stayed put, back home in Texas again—and still together.

Eileen figures her professional career matches her nomadic upbringing, since she's tried everything from drafting to a brief stint as a ranch hand—raising two children and any number of cats and dogs along the way. Not until she started writing did she "stay put," because that's when she knew she'd come home. Readers can write to her at P.O. Box 4612, Midland, TX 79704-4612.

DYNASTIES:
THE CONNELLYS

MEET THE CONNELLYS

Meet the Connellys of Chicago—
wealthy, powerful and rocked by scandal,
betrayal...and passion!

Who's Who in
EXPECTING...AND IN DANGER

Rafe Connelly—The hotshot computer whiz turned daddy-to-be wants it all—security, success, family. But is he using the woman to get the baby...or the baby to get the woman?

Charlotte Masters—The prim and prissy assistant finds herself on the run, pregnant and alone. How long can she deny her heart...and keep her secrets?

Lucas Starwind—For this remaining P.I. on the Connelly case, it's all about determination, prestige and honor.... Or is it really about revenge?

One

The Windy City was living up to its name the second time someone tried to kill her.

At least Charlotte thought they'd tried to kill her. Sprawled across the hood of a parked car, with panic pounding in her chest, her hip throbbing, her calf burning and her coat flapping in the wind, she couldn't be sure. Maybe the driver simply hadn't seen her.

"You all right, lady?"

She stirred and looked up at the concerned face of a tall black man with a gold ring in his nose, another in his eyebrow, a leather jacket and a Cubs cap on his apparently bald head. Several others had stopped on the busy sidewalk to stare and exclaim. She caught snatches of conversation—"Crazy drivers!" and "Must have been drunk…" and "Where's a cop when you need one?"

Not here, thank goodness. The last thing she needed was to draw the attention of the police.

"I'm fine," she said to the concerned and the curious. "Thank you for asking." She pulled herself together mentally as she climbed off the car. Her knees weren't sure of themselves, but after sorting through her aches, she concluded she wasn't badly hurt. The car had missed her, after all. Thanks to the wind.

Charlotte had been crossing the street—with the light, of course. She always crossed with the light. She'd finished her bagel two blocks back and had been holding on to the sack, which was destined for the next trash can. A strong gust had grabbed it right out of her hand. She'd turned, meaning to chase it down so she could dispose of it properly...and saw the car.

It had been headed right for her in spite of the red light that should have protected her. It had even seemed to speed up in that split second between the instant she'd seen it and the next, when her body had taken over, hurling her out of its path.

But maybe that was paranoia speaking. Although it wasn't really paranoia, was it, if there truly were people out to get you?

"You sure you're okay?" the man in the Cubs cap and nose ring asked. A hefty woman advised her to call the police; another suggested she go to the hospital; someone else thought she should get a lawyer, though what she'd do with one, he didn't say. Charlotte took a moment to assure them again that she was fine, though she grimaced over the ruined panty hose—four-ninety-five a pair, dammit—and the trickle of blood running down her leg.

She put a hand protectively on her stomach. A little wiggle inside assured her that all was well, and she drew a deep, relieved breath.

Her backpack. Oh, Lord, she couldn't afford to lose that. Where—? Kneeling, she spotted it halfway under the car and dragged it out. Her arms felt like overcooked spaghetti.

"Hey, you want me to call someone to come get you?" It was the Cubs fan.

"Thank you, but that won't be necessary." Standing with the backpack slung over her shoulder was a good deal harder than it should have been. Her knees weren't in much better shape than her spaghetti arms.

Surely it had been a freak accident.

"Better sit down a minute. You're pale as a ghost. Bleeding, too."

Irritation threatened to swamp good manners. She hated being fussed over. "I'm always pale. I'll take care of the scrapes at work."

"You got far to go?"

"Just up the block, at Hole-in-the-Wall."

He cast a dubious glance that way, which she perfectly understood. The restaurant was aptly named, an eyesore in an area that had once been solidly blue collar, but was skidding rapidly downhill. The neighborhood was seedy, a little trashy, not quite a slum...everything she'd fought so hard to leave behind.

"You ain't up to working yet," he informed her with that particular male brand of arrogance that scraped on her pride like fingernails on a chalkboard.

"I appreciate your concern, but it isn't necessary." She started limping down the sidewalk, hoping he would get the hint and go about his own business.

It didn't work. He kept pace with her. "Don't trip over your ego, sister. I'm not hitting on you. Don't care for teeny, tiny blondes with big mouths." He shook his head. "You sure talk fancy for someone who works at the Hole."

Her unwanted escort had a pleasant tenor voice with surprising resonance. "Do you sing?"

He gave her a startled glance. "Why?"

She sighed. Most of the time she managed to keep her unruly tongue under control, but every now and then it flew free. "I wasn't hitting on you, either. I don't care for bossy males. Your voice reminded me of a tenor I heard sing 'Ness'un Dorma.'"

"You listen to opera, but you work at Hole-in-the-Wall?"

"You recognize an aria from *Turandot*, but you poke holes in your body?"

"Smart-mouthed, too," he observed. "Why you working at the Hole?"

"For my sins." Which was all too literally true. But she was going to get things straightened out soon, she promised herself for the fortieth time. Somehow.

They'd arrived at the steps that led down to the kitchen. She thanked her escort as politely as she could manage, hobbled down and pushed the door open.

The kitchen was a long, narrow, crowded room. The cook, a stringy old man with limited notions of personal hygiene, gave her a sour look. "Better get moving. Zeno's in a bad mood."

"How can you tell?"

He snorted. "You go right ahead and smart off to him today like you been doin'. You'll see." He went back to flipping hamburger patties.

Charlotte hobbled to the cubbyhole where employees could leave their things. Dammit, she really did need to mind her tongue. She needed this job, and the Hole—for all its obvious drawbacks—did have three things in its favor. First, it was within walking distance of the cupboard-size apartment she'd found. Second, Zeno was allergic to cigarette smoke, so the entire place was smoke-free. Third, he was sloppy about paperwork and regulations—a definite drawback in terms of health and safety regulations, but a plus for her personally. He hadn't called any of the bogus references she'd listed on her application, and he didn't question her social security card—a good thing, since the number wasn't hers.

A man who was running a bookie operation out of his restaurant really ought to be more scrupulous about following the rules in his legitimate business, she thought as she slung her backpack under the table. She pulled off her coat, giving the shabby, shapeless brown material a look of distaste as she hung it on a hook. Best not to think about the beautiful new cream-colored wool coat hanging in the closet in her apartment—her old apartment.

The rent was paid up until the first. They won't have

sold her things yet, she told herself. Maybe she would still be able to get them back.

"You're late," a deep voice growled from the doorway. "Shift starts at five, not whenever you get around to showing up."

She jumped, scowled and looked at the doorway. Zeno stood there glowering at her. He was a man who could glower well. The paunch, thick eyebrows and bristly jowls gave him a head start in the mean-and-nasty sweepstakes.

Watch what you say, she reminded herself, and reached for the dusty first aid box on the top shelf. "A car nearly ran me down at the light."

"Late's late. It happens again, you're out of here."

"I would have been a lot later if the car had hit me." She gave the cap on the peroxide bottle an angry twist. "And yes, I'm all right, thank you so much for asking."

"If you're all right, you can get your butt out there and take orders."

"As soon as I've wiped the blood off. I'm pretty sure it's a health code violation for me to bleed on the customers." *Stop that,* she told herself. Zeno was not the kind of tyrant who admired those who stood up to him. He preferred quivering timidity. She pressed her lips together and began to clean the long scrape on her calf.

"Maybe I didn't explain when I hired you. I hate attitude. What I like is 'yes, sir, no, sir, right away, sir.' Got that, you stupid— What the hell do you want?" He turned on the waitress who'd come up behind him, a doe-eyed young woman named Nikki—"with two *k*'s and an *i*," she'd told Charlotte when they were introduced. Like Charlotte, she was blond. All of Zeno's waitresses were blond. Nikki was the kind the jokes were made for, though.

"Mr. Jones wants to talk to you," Nikki said nervously. "Table twelve."

"Why the hell didn't you say so? And *you*, Madame Attitude—" he jabbed a thick finger in her direction "—you've got five minutes to get out on the floor, or you're fired."

She tried to make herself say "yes, sir," but the words wouldn't come out. She'd said them to her former boss a thousand times, said them easily, naturally. Because he was a man who deserved her respect. Her throat closed up. Grant Connelly wouldn't care about her respect. Not now. Not after what she'd done.

She managed to nod stiffly. Zeno gave her one last glare and stomped off. Charlotte threw the bloody swab in the trash.

"What happened to you, anyway?" Nikki asked, her eyes big.

"I had a little accident on the way here. Stand in the doorway so no one comes in, would you?" She had no doubt Zeno had meant what he said about firing her if she wasn't on the floor in five minutes. Her panty hose would have to come off right here. Charlotte grimaced, but accepted necessity.

Nikki obligingly stood in the center of the narrow doorway while Charlotte took off her shoes, then reached up under her skirt to pull down the ruined panty hose. Her legs were going to freeze on the walk back to her overpriced cupboard when her shift was over...but cold legs were the least of her problems.

"Zeno's sure on a tear. You'd better put your apron on."

"It's pink." She pitched the panty hose in the trash, fumbled her shoes on and grabbed her order book. "I don't do pink."

"We're supposed to wear the aprons."

"I know." Nikki wasn't a bad sort—a bit dim, and with all the backbone of cotton candy, but nice enough. Charlotte found a smile for her. "Come on, let's get on the floor before I'm fired." She moved out into the kitchen, Nikki trailing behind.

"I guess you're worried that the baby will show if you tie the apron around your waist, huh?"

She froze. "I don't... What are you talking about?"

"Oh, c'mon. I mean, you're not showing much, but there's that little bulge, isn't there? And when Serena sneaks a smoke in the kitchen, you turn green. My sister Adrienne was the same way when she was carrying my nephew.''

Charlotte got her breath back, but couldn't make herself turn around. "Zeno's allergic to cigarette smoke, and I'm pretty sure *he* isn't pregnant."

Nikki giggled. "If he was, he'd be having triplets, wouldn't he? How far along are you?"

Sighing, Charlotte turned around. Her cover had been blown by a pink apron. "Five months. Please, if Zeno finds out, he'll—''

"As if I would! Tell Zeno? What kind of person do you think I am?"

"Sorry. I can't help worrying. I need this job."

"Then we'd better get moving." Nikki gave her a gentle shove and they headed for the stairs at the back of the kitchen. The restaurant's seating was on ground level, the kitchen in the basement. She'd be going up and down those steps a hundred times tonight.

"I guess it's scary when you're on your own," Nikki said. "Did the father walk out on you?"

Was flying to the other side of the country the same as walking out? Maybe not, since he didn't know about the baby. All at once Charlotte was dead tired. Everything was wrong, and she couldn't seem to make any of it come right again.

Not everything, she reminded herself. At least she knew Brad was safe. Probably. As long as no one knew where he was. "We shouldn't talk about this here," she said. "Maybe you won't say anything, but if someone overheard…"

"Like that Serena." She nodded, making her platinum curls bob. "She'd split on you in a second. Good thing she never looks past her mirror."

Charlotte pushed open the swinging door. "True. Which station do I have tonight?"

"Four. Serena's on two, I've got one, and—hey, what's wrong?"

"Nothing." She hoped. "The tall guy with the shaved head and Cubs cap in my station. The one talking on a cell phone. Have you seen him in here before?"

Nikki cocked her head. "Don't think so. Why?"

Idiot. Why had she told him where she worked? "He said he didn't like teensy blondes," she muttered.

"Who, that guy? He's kinda cute." She cocked her head and smiled. "Maybe he likes tall blondes."

Had it been coincidence that he'd been there when the car nearly ran her down? He'd seemed nice, in a rude sort of way. But he'd insisted on walking with her, and now here he was.... Panic flared. She didn't know what to do, whether she should run or stay. Charlotte took a deep breath.

She had her backpack. If she had to—if he seemed too interested, or acted funny—she could be out the back door in a flash. "Want to swap stations? You could find out if he likes tall blondes better than dinky ones like me."

For the next half hour she tried to keep busy. But her nerves were jumping, and each minute jerked into the next in a painfully slow way. Her admirer—if that's what he was—didn't make any effort to talk to her. So why was he here? He wasn't a regular, and he hadn't spoken to Zeno, so he wasn't here to bet on the horses, or whatever.

Finally she couldn't stand it anymore. After delivering a French dip, a pastrami on rye and two hamburgers to the third table in her station, she went up to Mr. Cubs Cap.

"Okay," she said, trying to ignore the way her heart was pounding. "I want to know why you followed me here."

"Didn't." He pounded on the bottom of his ketchup bottle. "Your ego's showing again, sister. I was here, I was hungry, I decided to eat. Hey, you think you could get me some more ketchup? This one's about dry."

Automatically she took the bottle he held out. "I don't believe you."

"And I don't care. You going to get me some ketchup or not?"

A hand landed heavily on her shoulder. "Never mind, Dix. I'll take it from here."

In her dreams Charlotte had sometimes plummeted in an out-of-control elevator. That was what this felt like now—the stomach-dropping second of disbelief sliding into greasy fear and guilt. And, God help her, mixing with the swift kick of desire.

Her eyes closed. "Rafe," she whispered.

"Got it in one." His voice was cordial—and achingly familiar. His grip on her shoulder was tight. "I guess that means you haven't forgotten me entirely, even if a few other things have slipped your mind."

Slowly she turned. His hand fell away.

His trench coat was long, black and leather. His jeans had probably come from a discount store, but the dark blue shirt would be the finest Egyptian cotton because Rafe liked the way it felt. He'd told her that once. His wavy brown hair was too long, as usual, wild and shaggy. It looked as if the wind had been playing with it.

Or a woman. That, too, would be as usual.

He doesn't belong here, she thought with a rising sense of panic. He wasn't supposed to be here, not in a place like this. He was too blasted *perfect* for a place like this.

The thought gave her courage. Maybe it was a fool's version, born of anger and untainted by common sense, but she'd take what she could get. She straightened her shoulders. "I suppose you want to talk to me, but it will have to wait until my shift is over."

"No," he said slowly. "I don't think it will." He took her hand and started for the door, dragging her with him.

"Rafe." She tried to pull her hand free. "Have you lost your mind? I can't go with you now."

"Sure you can." He didn't slow as he wove through the crowded tables.

People were staring. She set her feet firmly so he couldn't keep tugging her along like a reluctant puppy, and for a moment it worked. He gave her a hard look over his shoulder and a sharp jerk on the hand imprisoned in his.

She nearly toppled. It was either stumble after him or fall to the floor. He dragged her another few steps. "Dammit, you're going to get me fired!"

"Do you think I give a flying—"

"What the hell is going on here?" Zeno planted himself in front of Rafe, glower firmly in place.

Charlotte had never imagined she would see Zeno in the light of a savior. "This idiot is dragging me out the door!"

"I don't want any trouble here," Zeno said, sparing her a condemning glance, as if it were all her fault this madman was trying to abduct her. "Whatever your problem with her is, you'll have to settle things when she's not working."

"She won't be working for you anymore after tonight," Rafe informed him calmly.

"Yes, I will." She gave one more hard tug, but only succeeded in hurting her wrist.

Rafe went on as if she hadn't spoken. "She shouldn't be working here now, not in her condition."

"What condition?" Zeno demanded.

Don't tell him, Charlotte chanted mentally. Don't tell him, please...

Rafe's eyebrows lifted. "You didn't know that she's pregnant?"

"She's *what?*" Zeno rounded on her. "Why, you lying little bitch. Is that why you've been wearing those puke-ugly sweaters?" He grabbed the hem of her sweater, pulled it tight, and put his hand on the bulge of her stomach.

Rafe dropped her hand. And swung once, clean, short and sharp, his fist connecting with Zeno's jaw with a solid thunk. The older man's eyes opened wide in amazement just before he collapsed.

Rafe rubbed his fist. "No touching," he growled. Then he grabbed Charlotte's hand and towed her out of there.

Two

_____

"Have you lost your mind?" she shrieked as he dragged her out the door. "You just punched out my boss!"

"Something tells me he isn't your boss anymore."

It was fully dark now—as dark as this corner of the city ever got, at least. The air was cold, the night punctuated with horns and headlights. Neon draped its tawdry glitter over buildings, cars and faces. Those faces were fewer than before and their owners moved more slowly, the ones in groups laughing too loudly, those alone wary and watchful. Or simply empty. The women's skirts were shorter, their lips brighter red. And none of the night people crowding the sidewalk seemed inclined to take exception to the man in a black leather trench coat who bullied his way through them, or the way he dragged his unwilling victim along.

She tried again to reason with Rafe. "It's cold. My coat…my things…you have to let me get my things." Her backpack, especially. She couldn't lose it.

"My car's just up the block. The heater works."

"You can't just drag me off this way! It—it's illegal."

"Yeah?" He stopped and turned so abruptly she plowed into him.

She landed with her free hand bracing her against his chest, preventing her from falling up against him, body to body. The leather coat was cool and supple beneath her hand. His chest was hard. So were his eyes, and the sarcastic curl of his lips wasn't a smile. She remembered the feel of that mouth on her and hastily pulled back.

"If you think I'm doing something illegal, you should yell for a cop." The curl grew into a sneer when she remained silent. "That's what I thought. Come on."

How Rafe had managed to find a parking spot right where he needed one, she didn't know. It was typical of the man, though. Luck, skill, karma—whatever force you credited, Rafe had more of it than any one man should. He had everything, from wealth and good looks to a successful career and a loving family. He should have been spoiled, shallow, dull. He wasn't. He was fascinating. Unaffected, unconventional, outgoing, generous.

The man's sheer perfection was the most irritating thing about him.

The hubcaps were still on his car, she noted as he shifted his grip to her arm and unlocked the door. But the car itself was not what Rafe Connelly was supposed to drive. He ought to have a dangerous, low-slung sports car, not a dark blue domestic sedan.

That was the second most irritating thing about Rafe—he never did what you expected him to do.

"Get in," he ordered as he swung the door open.

She sighed and did it. There was no point in arguing. He'd already gotten her fired, so she had little left to lose. They might as well get this over with. It wasn't going to be pleasant. She knew that. But she'd made it through a lot of life's unpleasant moments. She'd get through this one, too.

His car might not be the sports car that fit her image of him, but it was new and expensive. And familiar. She passed a hand over the cool leather of the seat and tried not to think about the only other time she'd ridden in Rafe's car.

He slid behind the steering wheel, slammed his door and started the engine. Sound poured from the speakers—some kind of rock with screaming guitars, lots of bass and a pounding beat. Cold air poured from the vents. No doubt his car did have a great heater, but the engine wasn't warm yet. She shivered and hugged herself for warmth.

With a flick of his wrist, he cut the stereo off. Silence fell. He glanced at her, grimaced, flung his door open again in defiance of the traffic, got out and shrugged off his coat. He tossed it at her and climbed back in without saying a word.

Charlotte drew the coat over her like a blanket. The lining held the heat from his body, and the warmth released scents that drifted up to tease her. Leather and man and memories... How unpredictable he was. First he dragged her along willy-nilly, then he gave her the coat off his back.

His voice was quiet. "It's mine, isn't it?"

He wasn't talking about the coat. Charlotte closed her eyes, but that petty escape didn't help. He was here, he was asking, and she had to face both him and the facts. "Yes."

He smacked the steering wheel with his fist. Hard.

She jumped.

"Did it at any point occur to you that I'd want to know? That I had the *right* to know?"

"I was going to tell you. When—when I could."

"And when would that have been? When my son graduated from high school, were you going to send me an announcement? Maybe hit me up for college tuition?"

She looked down. Beneath the enveloping coat, her hands were clasped tightly together. "It might be a girl," she muttered.

"What?"

Her head came up. She scowled at him. "It might be your *daughter* who graduates, not your son."

"Girl, boy, what does it matter? The point is, you're carrying my child. So of course you ran off and took a job at a dive so you could live hand-to-mouth, stay on your feet for hours, then walk home late at night. In *this* neighborhood.''

Her mouth twisted in bitter humor. She'd grown up in neighborhoods like this one. ''I can take care of myself.''

''And one helluva job you've done of it, too. Considering that the mob is gunning for you.''

She swallowed and didn't reply.

''Damn shame the way things worked out for you.'' He turned in his seat, leaning against the door so he could survey her. His hand tapped the back of the seat in a quick, restless rhythm. ''Selling out my father should have netted you a nice chunk of change, but you've ended up on the bottom of the food chain, haven't you?'' He shook his head in mocking sympathy. ''You should be more selective about your business partners in the future.''

''It wasn't like that,'' she said, low-voiced.

''No? You want to tell me what it was like, then?''

Her lips felt stiff, numb. She'd known this would be unpleasant, but she hadn't realized how bad it would be. She hadn't known he would assume she'd done it for money.

But why wouldn't he? It was absurd for her to believe he should have known better. Illogical. ''I told the police. That's why there's a contract on my life.''

He sighed and his hand stopped its restless tapping. For a long moment he didn't say anything. He just looked at her.

She tilted her chin up and looked right back at him. And found herself caught, trapped in the fascinating topography of his face.

His eyes were so deep-set the lids hardly showed. In this light his eyes looked black, as dark as the thick slash of his eyebrows, which were much darker than the medium brown of his shaggy hair. His beard, too, grew in dark, and there was a rakish trace of stubble on his cheeks tonight. His nose was straight and perfect, with that fascinating little dip beneath that inevitably led her eyes to his mouth. Oh, that mouth…it was a mouth made for smiles and kisses, the upper lip a perfect match for the lower. But it was entirely too sensual for the aristocratic nose, too wide for his narrow face, too frivolous for those dark eyes.

Rafe was composed of too many unmatched pieces. His parts shouldn't have added up to such an enticing whole, and she resented mightily that they did.

One corner of that enticing mouth kicked up. "You'd stare down a cat, wouldn't you?" He ran a hand over his head, further messing his hair. "Dix said someone nearly ran you down this evening."

Dix? Oh. Her surly Good Samaritan. "The man in the Cubs cap. He called you. He's working for you."

"Dix is a friend, but yeah, he's been working for me." A muscle jumped in his jaw. "Helping me find you. I've been trying to do that for months."

She rolled her eyes. "Oh, yes. You tried so hard."

"I called. You never called back."

"How could I forget? A month after climbing out of my bed, you did get around to leaving a message on my answering machine."

"I was out of town. You knew I had to leave the next morning. And I left several messages, dammit, not just one!"

Eventually, yes. He'd called three times. It had been too little, too late. "If you'd really wanted to talk to me, you knew where I was—until last month, at least."

"Yeah." His voice was flat. "Right there in my father's office, pretending to be his loyal assistant while you sold him out to the Kellys."

"So I'm slime." She stared straight ahead, determined not to cry. "You'd decided I wasn't worth the trouble long before you found out what I'd done."

He shifted, looking away. "It wasn't like that."

Right. She didn't want to hear whatever version of "you're just not my type" he'd cooked up to explain himself. She knew very well how little they had in common, aside from some combustible hormones. She'd known it all along.

And still she'd made a fool of herself with him. Tension knotted her jaw and neck. She took a deep breath, trying to relax those muscles. It didn't help. "How did you find me?"

"You used your mother's social security number at that dive I just rescued you from."

"Rescue? Is that what you want to call it?" Temper warmed her. She shoved his coat down into her lap. "And how would you know what number I used?"

He shrugged. "Dix can find pretty much anything that's in any computer file, anywhere."

"He's a hacker, you mean." She shook her head. Rafe never made sense. Why would a computer systems analyst who specialized in corporate security have a hacker friend?

"One of the best. I asked him to check the social security records of the family members listed in your personnel file at Connelly Corporation. Earnings have been recently reported under your mother's number—pretty amazing, considering she passed away nine years ago."

If Rafe could track her that way, so could others. Suddenly she wasn't warm anymore. "Maybe I'd better not go back to my apartment." That made two apartments she'd had to abandon.

"Congratulations. That's the first sensible thing you've said tonight."

But where would she go? She had only her tip money in her pocket; the rest was in her backpack, back at Hole-in-the-Wall. She needed to go back and get it, but two hundred and thirteen dollars wouldn't go far.

God. She was practically a street person. She knew what she had to do, but she hated it. Hated it. "I don't like to ask," she said, her throat tight, "but could you loan me some money? I don't have enough to get another place to stay."

Rafe didn't think he'd ever been this angry. Or this scared. He didn't like either feeling, but he especially hated the cramped, cold feeling in his chest he got when he thought about how close she had come to being hit by that car earlier.

Hell, he thought, dragging a hand through his hair. At the moment, he didn't like much of anything—not her, not himself and for damned sure not what he had to do about their situation.

There was one small consolation. She wasn't going to like the next part, either. "No, I won't loan you any damned money." He put the car in gear and pulled away from the curb.

Her voice stopped just short of shrill. "What are you doing?"

"I used to think you were fairly bright. Figure it out."

Good thing he'd kept an eye on her as well as the traffic. He managed to snag her arm and jerk her back before she could get the door open. "Uh-uh. Jumping out of a moving vehicle is not allowed."

He let go of her arm, but continued to divide his attention between her and the road. She might try it again when they stopped for a light. "Put your seat belt on."

Already she was taking deep breaths, getting herself back under control. Dammit. He wished he didn't enjoy it so much when she ruffled up like an outraged hen then carefully smoothed each bristly feather back into place. Perverse of him, and showed a sad lack of judgment. The woman was a liar and a crook, or at least in the pay of crooks. She'd betrayed his father. He needed to remember that.

"Rafe, I have to get my backpack before it's stolen," she said in that reasonable tone that always made him want to unbutton something. Not that she had any buttons showing right now, but she used to wear a lot of prim, buttoned-to-the-throat silk blouses to work. No doubt she'd thought covering everything up would keep the men she worked with from turning into ravening beasts.

Foolish of her. But Rafe had figured out long ago that most women had no idea how little it took to turn a man's thoughts to sex. Her prim blouses had just made him notice the way the silk shined and shifted over those soft, round, gorgeous breasts...breasts whose shape and texture he knew now.

He shook his head and tried to banish the memory. "Forget your backpack. I'll buy you another one."

"I don't want you to buy me anything. I want *my* backpack."

He eased to a stop at the light. "Listen, Charlie, someone tried to kill you on the way to your job. You can't go back there."

"Don't call me Charlie."

Her rebuke was automatic, he felt sure. As automatic as the way the nickname had slipped out. How many times had he called her that in the past two years, since she took over as his father's executive assistant?

He'd called her Charlie when he'd come inside her, too.

"All right, *Charlotte*," he said, hating the name and halfway hating her, too. "Put your seat belt on. It's not safe for the baby if you ride without one, and I'm not letting you make any escape attempts."

She scowled, scooped his coat out of her lap and twisted around to deposit it in the back seat. Either she was warm enough now, or she didn't want anything of his touching her. Or she didn't want anything slowing her down when she made her break for freedom. He tapped the steering wheel with one hand, ready to grab her with the other.

"Rafe, I agreed to talk with you. I did not agree to be abducted."

"Tough. You haven't done such a great job of protecting yourself and our baby, so I'm taking over."

"If you're thinking about—about the incident today, it may not mean anything. Heaven knows Chicago has plenty of bad drivers."

"I've always admired that tidy brain of yours. I wonder why you aren't using it. Maybe you don't think I can use my brain. Yeah, that's probably it. You think you can persuade me there's no connection between people trying to run over you, and people shooting at you.'' The light changed and he accelerated. ''That's too much of a stretch for me, I'm afraid.''

Her hands made small, frustrated fists in her lap. ''Take me back to Hole-in-the-Wall.''

''No.''

Her tongue darted out nervously to lick her lips. ''If you're thinking of taking me to the police, please don't. The other time—when I was shot at—that happened as I was leaving police headquarters. I think someone in the department tipped them off. I don't want to go in a safe house. I don't think I'd be safe.''

''Amazing. We agree about something. Now put your seat belt on, or I'll reach over and put it on you.'' For a supposedly sensible woman, she sure wasn't paying attention to sensible precautions. ''My apartment's in the Bucktown area. We'll probably run across any number of bad drivers on the way there.''

''Your *what?* No.'' She shook her head so hard her hair flew into her face. ''No, I am not going to your apartment.''

''You don't have any choice. God knows I don't have much choice, either.'' He took a deep breath. Might as well get it said. ''You're carrying my baby. We'll get married.''

''That's not funny.''

He gave a short bark of laughter. ''You think I'm joking? If so, the joke's on me.'' Humor faded, settling into grim determination. ''I hope you don't have your heart set on a big wedding, because we can't go that route. We'd be issuing an invitation to the hit man along with the guests. He's been remarkably unlucky so far, but we can't count on his bad luck continuing.''

She looked stunned—and not with joy, either. At least she wasn't trying to leap out of the moving car.

''No comment? Good. We'll get the blood tests tomorrow.''

''You don't want to marry me!'' she burst out. ''You don't want to get married at all.'' She rubbed the back of her neck as if her head might be hurting. ''If this is some kind of noble gesture, all right, then. You've made it. I hereby let you off the hook."

"I want my child."

She closed her eyes, sighed and leaned her head against the headrest. "I want you to be part of the baby's life. You don't have to marry me for that."

"I don't want a weekend now and then. I want my *child.* I want it all—3:00 a.m. feedings and diaper rash, school dances and college entrance exams." He shook his head. "Weird, isn't it? I had no idea I'd feel this way, so I can't blame you for being surprised. But there it is. I want to be a full-time daddy, so we have to get married."

The hand that had been rubbing her neck fell into her lap. "And if I refuse to marry you, what will you do? Will you try to take the baby away from me?"

He shot her an irritated glance. "You think I'm some kind of monster? The last thing I want is a custody battle. That's why I'm proposing. Look, you need me."

"I don't need anyone. And you don't want me. I mean, you don't want to marry me."

His eyebrows lifted. Did she think he didn't want her now? Wrong, but interesting. Maybe useful. "You're right about me not wanting to get married. I don't. But I wasn't raised to duck my responsibilities." Of course, his parents hadn't raised him to have unprotected sex, either. He still didn't understand how he could have been that careless.

He realized he was scowling and tried to lighten up. "If you're worried about the sex part, don't. We can make things work out there just fine."

Her stony expression suggested just the opposite. "I don't suppose it's necessary for you to actually like a woman to go to bed with her. I'm a little pickier. I'm not marrying a man who despises me."

He hadn't expected this to be easy. Charlie was nothing if not stubborn. "Whether you like it or not, you do need me right now. You're running from some pretty big bad guys, and you lack the resources to do it right. If I could find you at that dive, they can, too. It looks as if they already have.''

She chewed on her lip. It was a small enough sign of nerves, but welcome. He was getting to her. Good.

Rafe switched tactics slightly. Let her think she'd won a compromise from him. Women were crazy about compromises. ''Look, you don't have to say yes or no about marriage right away. Stay at my place, though. Let me protect you. Don't endanger my baby out of pride.''

Silence descended for long moments.

''All right,'' she said abruptly. ''I won't marry you, but I'll stay in your apartment for now.''

It was more than he'd expected from her this quickly. He frowned, chewing over her capitulation in his mind. Maybe she was a lot more scared than she'd admitted—but there was no point in asking her. You could put Charlie in a cage of tigers and she'd insist she was fine. Or else she had some plan in mind. Something devious.

It was probably a sign of depravity that he was looking forward to figuring out her scheme. And stopping her.

Rafe considered himself a simple man. Computers were the one place he enjoyed knots and puzzles. He worked hard because he liked his work, and, he admitted, because he had his share of Connelly ambition. He played hard, too, when he was in the mood, but he also relaxed just as completely. He got more complexity than he needed from his big, maddening, high-profile family. When it came to his personal life, he kept things simple.

So how had he ended up in such a messy relationship with such a complicated woman?

There were her breasts, of course. He stole a sideways glance at her. Truly excellent breasts—not especially large, but beautifully shaped. And Charlie was great fun to tease—she always rose to his bait, but not always in the way he expected. She gave as good as she got, too. But while great breasts and teasing might account for his initial interest, they didn't explain why he'd taken her to bed the second he'd had the chance. Not when he'd known—dammit, he'd *known*—that she was a regular porcupine of complications.

She fascinated him. She was so charmingly tidy yet mysterious, keeping her private self tucked out of sight. He supposed a woman like Charlie needed to keep her externals orderly in order to cope with her complicated interior.

Yet in spite of her reserve he'd thought he knew her. Not all of her, maybe, but enough to like her. To trust her. Hell, his father had trusted her, and Grant Connelly was rarely wrong about that sort of thing.

Why had she done it? Why had she betrayed his father's trust?

He knew damned little. Last Christmas his oldest brother, Daniel, had surprised everyone, including himself, by becoming the heir to the throne of Altaria, the tiny Mediterranean country their mother hailed from. Almost immediately, someone had tried to kill him. Grant Connelly had hired a pair of private detectives—Lucas Starwind and Tom Reynolds—to look into the matter, but neither they nor the police had made much headway. They knew the attempt had been carried out by a pro, and that it was related to Daniel's new royal status. And that was about all they knew.

In May the Connelly Corporation computers had suffered a major crash. No surprise there. Rafe had been urging his father to upgrade his system for the past two years. At the time, Rafe had been involved with a big project in Phoenix. There had been no way he could take on another job. Charlie had suggested a technician who was familiar with the system and programs used at the corporation, and the tech seemed to have fixed things easily.

He'd fixed things, all right.

There had been no reason to suspect a link between a computer crash and the assassination attempt on Daniel. Not until last month. A connection had turned up then—a dead man.

Someone had murdered Tom Reynolds, one of the private detectives investigating the Connelly troubles. His body had been found in the alley behind the office of the computer tech who had restored the Connelly Corporation's system after the crash. And shortly before he was killed, Reynolds had called Grant to suggest that the corporate computer system needed to be checked out.

The technician himself had disappeared.

Charlie was the link between the tech and Connelly Corporation, and the police had picked up her up for questioning. At first she'd refused to talk in spite of the fact that Grant Connelly didn't want charges pressed against her. Then, as she was leaving police headquarters, someone had nearly managed to put a bullet between her eyes.

She'd talked after that—and then she'd vanished. Rafe couldn't find out much about what she'd told the police. They were being disgustingly closemouthed on that subject. All he knew was that Angie Donahue, the mother of his half-brother Seth, had somehow persuaded Charlie to use that particular technician.

And Angie Donahue was connected to the Kelly crime family.

Now there was a price on Charlie's head.

It all added up to one big, deadly mess. Rafe had canceled his next job, finished up the last one and flown home as soon as he could. Ever since, he'd been trying to find out what the tech had done to the corporate computers—when he wasn't trying to find Charlie.

City lights streamed past the windows on one side. On the other side the vast darkness of Lake Michigan was blocked by hotels and office buildings, with an occasional empty space giving a glimpse of the lake, spotted here and there by the running lights of freighters.

He glanced at the woman beside him. She was staring out the windshield as if she'd forgotten he existed. She'd been silent a long time. Dammit, he just knew she was coming up with new complications for him to sort out. "Does it move sometimes?" he asked abruptly.

"What?" She turned toward him, her eyes blank, as if she'd been far away.

"The baby. Do you feel it moving sometimes?"

"Oh." Her hand pressed her stomach, the fingers spreading as if she already had a big belly to support instead of a little bulge. A smile slipped over her face, changing it, making her look softer than he'd ever seen her. "Yes. She or he is asleep right now, I think, but I've been feeling movement for about a month now. It feels…" She shook her head, her expression full of wonder. "I don't know how to say it."

"It's a good feeling, though? It doesn't hurt or anything?"

Her glance was almost shy. She nodded. "It's good."

"Will you tell me the next time you feel it move? I'd sort of like to feel it, too."

Her cheeks flushed and she tucked her chin down as if he'd asked for something intensely personal. "I guess so."

"Good." He thought a minute. Maybe agreeing to let him share the baby before it was born was an intimacy she hadn't planned on. So he added, "Thank you."

She nodded and fell silent again.

Oh, she was going to make things difficult, he knew. She probably couldn't help it—she was a difficult woman. But he had some complications of his own in mind for her.

Charlie didn't want to marry him, but she had to. For her sake, his sake, and most of all for the sake of the life she was carrying. So he'd persuade her. Rafe knew just how to go about that—the same way he'd gotten himself into this mess.

He'd seduce her.

Three

Charlotte hadn't known what to expect of Rafe's apartment. She'd been pretty sure it wouldn't resemble his parents' home on Lake Shore Drive. Grant and Emma Connelly lived in a Georgian-style manor furnished in antiques and elegance, with landscaped grounds that included an ornamental pool and a boxwood maze. It was altogether gracious and tasteful, not to mention intimidatingly rich.

But Rafe wouldn't be interested in gracious or traditional. He was fond of the casual, the eclectic, the downright odd. So she hadn't been surprised when they'd arrived at a converted office building in an area that was as much commercial as residential. But still…

Whatever she'd unconsciously expected, she thought as she stood in the middle of Rafe's living space, *this* wasn't it. She rubbed the back of her head, where the threatened headache had settled, and turned in a slow circle, taking it all in.

Except for the kitchen, the entire downstairs was one big

room. The floor was wooden, the ceiling high, the colors bold. Furniture and floor treatments rather than walls defined the spaces. A change from wood to tile marked the dining area, which was anchored by an enormous painting of a jester, complete with whimsical hat, tasseled costume and airborne balls of many colors.

A sectional sofa in glowing apricot created an L-shaped conversational area in front of a fireplace. The fireplace itself was modern and white; the wall that held it had been painted deep blue. That same wall also held bookshelves, three windows, a stereo and a huge-screen TV. Facing the TV were cushy chairs upholstered in green and yellow and purple. A hammock swung gently in front of the single big window on the right-hand wall. Next to it was an iron staircase flanked by a stunning wooden statue of a nude woman.

"You have a strange look on your face," he said. "If you don't like the place, blame my sister Alexandra. She picked out most of the furniture."

She stopped looking at Rafe's things and looked at Rafe. He stood in the middle of all that color, looking dark and dangerous and out of place in his beard stubble and shaggy hair. In this light, the color of his eyes wasn't black, but blue—dark blue, like a stormy sky. "There's a tie on your chandelier," she said.

He glanced up, surprised. "So there is."

A bubble of laughter rose in spite of her aching head. She turned away, fighting a smile. The room was classy, expensive, extravagant—and extravagantly messy. Things were everywhere they didn't belong. Books, magazines, newspapers, clothing. A guitar. Two big, thoroughly dead plants. Computer parts were strewn across the glass-topped dining table, along with more papers, a pair of socks and a tool chest. The leather coat he'd loaned her was tossed across a low hassock. The wooden nude by the stairs wore a plastic lei and a Cubs cap.

She found the clutter oddly endearing. Rafe had always seemed like too much of a good thing—too sexy, too rich, too confident. His bright, sloppy apartment made him more human. Something warmed and softened inside her.

He sighed. "It's a mess, isn't it?"

"Ah…" She hunted for something tactful to say, but came up empty and settled for honesty. "Yes."

"Messy doesn't bother me, but you like things tidy. I'll see what I can do tomorrow." He glanced around, frowning as if he wasn't at all sure what that might be. "It is clean. You don't have to worry about that. Doreen comes at least once a week when I'm in town, and the woman is a demon on dirt. She'll clean anything that doesn't get out of her way. Nearly vacuumed me once when I was taking a nap, but fortunately I woke up in time."

Oh, the smile was winning, damn him. She bent to straighten a leaning pile of newspapers. "Were you napping in the hammock?"

"It's a restful spot. You don't need to do that."

"I can't help myself. What's behind the red wall?"

"The kitchen. There's also a half bath down here. The full bath is upstairs, along with my bedroom and office."

"And the guest room? Where I'll be staying—is that upstairs or down?"

"Ah…" He rubbed the back of his neck. "There isn't exactly a guest room. I used that for my office."

Temper made her head pound. "If you think I'm going to climb into your bed—"

"You'll be there alone…if that's what you want."

She refused to dignify that bit of blatant provocation with a reply. Turning, she headed for the stairs.

The rooms upstairs were smaller than down, but still much larger than the living room of her old apartment. A glance through the first open door revealed a room that was mostly high-tech office, though piles of papers and odds and ends of workout equipment hid some of the computer paraphernalia.

A glance through the opposite doorway made her smile and step inside.

His bathroom was long and narrow, walled in cobalt-blue tile, with gleaming white fixtures and a large shower stall bricked in glass blocks. That long wash of blue ended at a square, step-up tub deep enough to drown in. "Oh, my." She went straight for the tub. "I think I'm in love."

Rafe stood in the doorway. "Who would have thought it? The efficient Ms. Masters is a closet sybarite."

"Just a bathtub sybarite." And Rafe had her dream bathroom. She sighed in pleasure and envy and glanced over her shoulder. "So why are the towels hung up instead of dumped on the floor?"

"Childhood trauma. My mother was fierce on the subject of damp towels left on the floor. You want to take a bath before we eat? It might help that headache you've been nursing."

Her eyebrows twitched in surprise. "How did you know I've got a headache?"

"I'm psychic. And you're rubbing your head again."

She blinked and dropped her hand self-consciously.

His grin flashed. "Come on. I'll get you something to change into." He vanished into the short hall, his voice reaching her easily. "I'll fix dinner while you soak. Steaks okay?"

"Don't go to any trouble." She followed, confused by his shifting moods and wondering about the condition of his kitchen, given what she'd seen of the rest of the place. "Sandwiches or takeout would be..." Speech and feet both drifted to a halt when she reached his bedroom.

At first all she saw was the bed—huge, unmade, with tousled sheets, scattered pillows, and the comforter dragging the floor at one corner. It looked much the way her bed had on one morning five months ago.

Had someone shared that bed with him recently?

He spoke, drawing her attention to his amused face. "Don't worry. The mere sight of a bed won't make me pounce on you."

"Why bother?" she muttered. "Been there, done that."

As soon as the words were out, she cursed her slippery tongue. "I didn't say that."

"Yes, you did. You're thinking of the last time we were in a bedroom together."

"No." Memories pressed at her, an insistent thrust of heat and haste and impulse. The flavor of his mouth. The feel of his hands, quick and demanding. And her own dizzy need rising to meet those demands. "Not at all."

"I am. I'm remembering the way you taste when your pulse is pounding here." He lifted a hand and touched his own throat beneath the jaw.

Her own hand lifted involuntarily, mirroring his gesture, and quickly dropped. Her pulse *was* pounding. Dammit. "I don't care to wander down memory lane tonight. I'd rather wash the grime off."

"Why do I like that cool, sarcastic mouth of yours so much?" He shook his head. "Hell if know."

His lips were smiling. His eyes weren't. They were dark, intent. Hot. Oh, she knew that expression, was as fascinated by it tonight as she had been five months ago. As fascinated as birds are said to be by the gaze of a snake. That's superstition, she told herself. And couldn't keep from falling back a step when he moved toward her.

His smile widened. "Your nightie," he said, and held out what she only then noticed he held—an old sweat suit. "I told you I wouldn't pounce, but if you get the urge, feel free to jump on me."

"In your dreams."

His mouth still curved in that infuriating, knowing smile. "Oh, you have been, Charlie. You have been."

Her mouth went dry. Something fluttered in her chest—something too much like yearning. She snatched the clothes from him and escaped with as much dignity as possible.

The air was warm and moist, the water warmer and soothing. Her hair smelled of almonds from Rafe's shampoo. Charlotte lathered her left leg, then drew the razor along her calf.

This bathroom might have been conjured out of one of her private fantasies. *Oh, admit it,* she thought. The entire apartment seemed to belong in one of her daydreams, not her real life.

Except for the mess. Her mouth curved. She'd never pictured her dream apartment with so many piles of misplaced objects. Or a hammock. But the expensive furnishings, the artful use of color and space, the curving iron staircase and fireplace and beautiful rugs—she'd dreamed of a place like this, possessions like these, for years.

Charlotte had a hunger for nice things. *A product of my deprived childhood,* she thought with bitter humor, dipping her leg beneath the water to rinse. It wasn't a quality she admired in herself, but she accepted it. Possessions would probably always matter a little too much to her.

She leaned against the back of the tub. Had he really dreamed of her?

It didn't matter. It couldn't matter, she told herself fiercely. She knew better than to confuse fantasy with reality. Maybe he *had* dreamed of her. They'd been incredibly good together in bed. But dreams weren't a guide for real life, and great sex wasn't a basis for a marriage.

In dreams, she thought, her eyes drifting closed, anything could happen.

Someone rolled over inside her.

Her hand went to her stomach. It amazed her every time, this motion created by another being right inside her body. Would she grow used to the sensation in the next four months? Would she be more grouchy than awed when the baby was bigger and woke her up at night, kicking?

She smiled. She didn't think so. Much to her surprise, she loved being pregnant. Oh, at first she'd been scared and nauseous, appalled that this could happen to her, that she could have been so irresponsible. But the first time the baby had moved...she rubbed her middle, smiling, her eyes still

closed. Now she even liked the way her body was expand-
ing, the solid shape the baby made inside her. After being
alone in her body all her life, she couldn't stop marveling
at being two instead of one.

Funny. She'd never dreamed about being pregnant, yet
now that she was, she loved it. Her fantasies had usually
revolved around success in some form. Stock options. A
well-fed 401K. Beautiful things of all sorts, from handmade
quilts to designer suits to a hopeless craving she'd suffered
from for months for an antique rolltop desk.

Though there had been another dream…. No, that was
too important a word for her foolishness. A silly fantasy,
that was all it had been. It had seemed harmless. She'd
worked at the Connelly Corporation for three years and as
Grant's assistant for two, and Rafe had never asked her out.
She'd been sure he never would, sure her longing would
go safely unrequited…until the night five months ago when
the Connellys had held a barbecue at their lakeside cottage.

She'd gone there to get Grant's signature on a contract.
And Rafe, damn his observant eyes, had realized something
was bothering her. Grabbing at the first excuse that had
come to mind, she'd claimed to be ill. Big mistake. Grant
had refused to hear of her driving back to work. He'd refused to hear of her driving at all.

Rafe had offered to take her home. And she, foolish
dreamer that she'd been, hadn't protested nearly enough….

One night in May

"So what's wrong?" Rafe asked as they headed back to
the city on Lake Shore Drive.

"Just a bug, I guess." Outside, the air was dreamy with
dusk. To their left, the vast waters of Lake Michigan were
turning gray and secretive in the fading light. There were
secrets inside the car, too. They pressed on Charlotte,

weighed her down, made her want to be anywhere but here, with this man.

She leaned her head against the headrest and tried to relax. The ride was smooth and quiet, the leather seats absurdly comfortable. But the tension vibrating inside her wouldn't let go. "I'd pictured you with a sporty little two-seater."

"If I get the urge to travel with my knees jammed up to my chest, I fly economy class. No need to buy a car that does that for me."

A smile tugged at her mouth. Rafe had a way of making her smile, making her angry, making her feel all sorts of things she didn't want to feel. "I'll bet you've never flown economy in your life."

"You'd lose." He signaled and slowed the car. "I don't think you're sick."

She sat up straight. "What a strange thing to say. Unless your ego is crowding out your brain, and you think I lured you away from the party to have my wicked way with you."

He chuckled. "Don't I wish. No, you did your best to get out of accepting a ride. You've got an annoyingly large independent streak, Charlie."

"My name is Charlotte," she corrected him automatically, looking down at her lap. Her fingers rested there calmly enough, but inside she was rattling like a poorly tuned engine. There was a giddy intimacy in riding in Rafe's car, alone with him as darkness eased up on the city. But this pull she felt was the last thing she needed right now. It distracted her. She needed to be thinking about how to find out what that tech had done so she could undo it, not about the way Rafe's forearms looked with his sleeves rolled up.

He glanced at her, his grin flashing. "Nervous about being alone with me?"

"Don't be silly."

"If Dad hadn't been there to bully you, you'd never have gotten in this car with me."

"Your father doesn't bully. He's been very good to me." And in return, she'd betrayed him. But what else could she have done? Oh, Brad, she thought, miserable in her love and guilt. Somehow she would make things right again. If she had to go to the office every weekend, she'd make things right.

For everyone else, a little voice inside whispered. She might be able to put things right for others, but her own dreams were forever spoiled. There never had been any chance of a future for her and Rafe, she reminded that whispery voice. They were too different. Besides, he liked to tease, he liked to flirt, but he'd had three years to fall for her, if he was going to.

Obviously he wasn't.

She kept her eyes closed, faking the sleep her unquiet mind wouldn't allow. Rafe either believed she'd dozed off or was willing to let the conversation drift to an end. Neither of them had spoken for perhaps fifteen minutes when he broke the silence. "Here we are."

She straightened, frowning as he pulled to a stop. "*Where* are we?"

"A couple blocks from a great Italian restaurant." He turned off the engine, got out and came around to her side. She remained where she was, flustered and angry. When he opened her door she said, "I'm not in the mood for a kidnapping."

"This isn't a kidnapping. I'm taking you to dinner."

"I don't recall being asked."

"If I'd asked, you'd have said no. Look, Charlie, you're not sick. You just said that because you didn't want to talk about whatever has you upset. Man problems, probably. But I'm not a bad listener. You might try not holding everything in, see if it helps."

Oh, yes, he was just the person for her to confide in. *You see, gangsters forced me to let them do something to the computers at your family's corporation....*

"No," she said firmly. "Thank you, but no. I'll be fine."

He nodded. "That's what I thought. You look like a woman in need of a good cry, but you aren't about to let your hair down and take advantage of my broad, manly shoulders, are you? So I decided to feed you instead. Tony makes great lasagna."

To her alarm, the quivering inside threatened to spill outside. She bit her lip to keep it steady. "I'm sure you know a lot about women, but I don't think you know much about the therapeutic effects of a good cry."

"I've got sisters." He heaved a huge sigh. "Lord, do I have sisters."

"Three sisters might make you seem like a poor, outnumbered male if you didn't also have five brothers."

"Seven brothers now."

Of course. She felt like a fool for forgetting. Rafe had grown up with five brothers, including a half brother, but last month the family had learned of two more Connelly men—twins, the product of a youthful affair of Grant's that had taken place before he married Emma.

A discovery like that might have torn another family apart. Not the Connellys. Oh, there had been some turmoil. She'd heard raised voices in Grant's office a couple of times, but that sort of thing happened from time to time anyway, and meant little. The Connellys were stubborn, strong-minded people, every one of them. Sometimes they were angry and loud. But the storms came and went, leaving the family still solid. United.

What would it be like to have such a family? So many, and so close. There would always be someone to listen, to help if you needed it.... The squeeze of something horribly close to self-pity made her voice sharper than she intended. "You prove my point. Testosterone seven, estrogen three. The testosterone count wins."

"Come on. You've met my sisters. Can you really believe any of us poor males ever wins?"

She chuckled in spite of herself.

"That's better." He reached in and took her hand. "Come on, Charlie. Eat. You'll feel better. If you're good, I'll even spring for tiramisu."

Charlotte lay in the cooling water, remembering the crowded little restaurant, the wobbly table covered by a cheap vinyl tablecloth and the incredible lasagna. They'd shared a bottle of wine while they talked, teased and argued. And she'd forgotten to worry. Or maybe she'd willfully shoved worry aside, seizing the chance to feel good with both hands, like a greedy child.

Rafe had taken her home. He'd insisted on walking her up to her apartment. At her door he'd kissed her...and all those dreams, all those foolish, impractical dreams had blazed to life along with her body.

She remembered the look in his eyes when he'd lifted his head. The way she'd felt when his hand sifted through her hair. His hand hadn't been entirely steady, and she'd let herself hope. For a moment hope had bloomed in her, bright and mute as sunrise.

Maybe he'd seen it in her eyes, because she remembered very clearly what he'd said. "I want to come in, Charlie. I want to be with you. But we need to be clear with each other." That gentle hand had cradled her head, his thumb spread to stroke her temple. "No expectations beyond what we can give each other tonight."

She'd let him in. Even as those silent hopes died, she'd let him in, wanting passion and memories, craving whatever temporary oblivion he might bring her.

Rafe had been a skilled lover, and a greedy one. And he'd left before sunrise. She'd pretended to sleep while he found his clothes in the dark. Even when he'd bent over her and his lips had brushed her cheek, she'd faked sleep, afraid that if she spoke, if she did anything to acknowledge his leaving, she would embarrass them both.

No expectations. He'd wanted to be with her, but once had been enough.

She sighed once and stood, reaching for one of the thick, oversize towels. He had at least left her a note. She'd burned it.

The blasted towel smelled like him. She made a face and rubbed herself dry briskly. None of that, she told her excitable hormones. Since the night when she'd tumbled into bed with him so easily, she'd done a much better job of shutting out foolish dreams. In fact, she hardly dreamed at all anymore.

Four

Rafe was using his favorite knife on a fresh shitake mushroom when he heard Charlie coming down the iron staircase. She'd spent an ungodly amount of time in the bathroom, but he'd expected that. He'd once asked his sister Maggie what women did in bathtubs that took so long. She'd given him one of those ''I Am Woman'' superior looks and told him he wouldn't understand.

Women and bathtubs. He shook his head and got the steaks out of the refrigerator, where they'd been marinating. The broiler was already hot. He was forking the steaks onto the broiler pan when she spoke.

''You're cooking!''

''I said I would.''

''No, I mean *really* cooking. I smell herbs—oregano?— and you're cutting up vegetables.''

''Vegetables for the salad, oregano and rosemary in the marinade for the steaks.'' He closed the oven door and glanced at her. Then paused, startled. ''Your hair is curly.''

Her hand lifted self-consciously to touch the damp curls. "I couldn't find a blow-dryer, so I towel-dried it."

"I don't have one." He couldn't stop staring. She looked so pretty with her face all warm and pink from her bath and her hair all messy with curls. His sweats pretty much swallowed her, of course. She'd rolled up the sleeves and the pant legs several times. "You always wear your hair all smoothed out." He shook his head. "It looks nice smooth, but I like it like this. Curly and a little wild."

"I like it smooth." She wandered around, inspecting his kitchen with a small, worried vee between her eyebrows. "I had no idea you knew how to cook. Your kitchen—" She waved one hand at the counter. "Everything's clean. Not just wiped-down clean, but put-away clean. The rest of your place is a mess, but the kitchen is neat. And you've got enough pots hanging in the pot rack to open a kitchen supply store."

Her consternation made him smile. "We're learning a lot about each other. I thought your hair was straight. You thought I couldn't cook." He shook his head sadly. "I had no idea you were sexist."

"Most men *don't* cook." When he lifted an eyebrow, she added with dignity, "That's an observation, not a sexist comment. And your family...you must have grown up with a cook."

"I remember one of them—Abraham. He gave me great advice when I was in college. Women are turned on by a man who cooks for them."

Her mouth made a small, disgusted moue. "I should have known." Moving to the chopping board, she picked up the knife, finished slicing the mushroom and reached for a carrot.

"You like to cook, too?" He moved closer, stopping behind her. His shampoo sure smelled different on her than it did on him. He bent to sniff.

Her hand stilled. "Sometimes. I do know how to use a knife."

"Threats. How exciting." He lifted a strand of that damp hair and let it curl across his palm in a soft question mark. "Want to slip into something leather and say that again?"

The muffled sound she made might have been a laugh, quickly stifled. "Anyone ever tell you you're easy?"

"I hear it all the time." He released the strand of hair he'd been toying with and let his fingertips trace the soft skin along the side of her neck. "Anyone ever tell you your skin feels like rose petals?"

"Rafe." Her shoulders stiffened. "Don't."

He didn't want to stop. He wanted to bend and nuzzle the warm place where her neck met her shoulder. To slide his hands up beneath the sweatshirt and find out if she was wearing a bra, or if she'd left herself deliciously bare. She had such beautiful breasts. He wanted to see them again, taste them.

He wanted it—wanted her—a little too much.

When he stepped back, his heart was pounding. He was as hard as if he'd been playing with her breasts instead of thinking about them. It was ridiculous, alarming, to be this aroused this quickly. He cleared his throat. "What's your preference? I like medium rare myself, and I'm warning you I have moral objections to well-done."

Her head moved back and forth in a single confused shake. "Well-done what?"

"It's a sin to ruin a good T-bone by cooking it into leather."

"Oh. The steaks." At last her hand completed the motion she'd started moments before, and she started slicing the carrot. "Medium, please."

There was a husky note in her voice. It was some consolation to know she'd been affected, too. But not a lot. He scowled as he went to the pantry, where he grabbed a bottle of rosé. "Are you allowed to have wine?"

"Best if I don't." Her voice was already back to normal. Oh, she was a cool one, Charlie was—except for that hair. The drier it got, the friskier it got. It looked like scrambled sunlight now, a messy red-gold riot skimming her shoulders.

This was why he'd never asked Charlie out, he thought. Why he'd teased and flirted and argued with her, and been careful to never see her outside his father's office. She stirred him, yes. That part was fine. But there was something else, something about her that set off all kinds of warning bells. She was too complicated, kept too much of herself hidden. A woman like that could get her hooks in a man so deep he'd never be free again.

It was a little late for him to worry about his freedom, wasn't it?

"So what do you want to drink?" he snapped. "I'm going to have wine."

Her glance was puzzled. "Fine. Milk would be great for me, if you have some. Or water."

"I've got milk." Rafe jabbed the corkscrew in. He'd slipped the noose around his neck himself when he took her to bed, and she'd been bothering him ever since. The blasted woman kept showing up in his thoughts when she had no business being there. And now—*now* she had the gall to say she didn't want to marry him. He gave the corkscrew a vicious twist.

"The salad's ready. What kind of dressing do you want?" she asked, moving to the refrigerator.

"There's fresh vinaigrette in a bottle in the door. What kind of ring do you want?"

She frowned. "Is that what soured your mood all of a sudden—thinking of wedding rings? Cheer up. I'm not marrying you."

He looked at the slight bulge of her belly beneath the sweats, the round breasts and the drying curls that were so different from the in-control image she liked to present to the world.

In bed, Charlie lost control. Soon, he promised himself,

he would begin uncovering some of those secrets she hoarded so zealously. "You may not plan to, but you will, Charlie. You will."

It was a strained meal. The food was delicious, and Charlotte ate more than she'd expected to. But the company lacked a certain something. Like the ability to carry on a conversation.

Usually Rafe's moods were easy to read. When he was angry, he exploded. When he wanted to charm, he charmed. Happy, gloomy, tired, funny—his thoughts might be a mystery, but whatever he felt was usually right out there for all to see. But usually he talked. Whatever his mood was tonight, it involved a lot of silence. The monosyllabic replies she received when she tried to start a conversation annoyed her into her own silence.

For a man who claimed he wanted to marry her, he certainly didn't seem interested in speaking to her.

She escaped to the kitchen as soon as possible, insisting that since he'd cooked she would handle the cleanup. He gave her an unsmiling glance, shrugged and told her to have fun. When she finished loading the dishwasher, he was nowhere in sight. She glanced at the stairs and caught the faint sound of the shower running.

She would stay down here, then.

Her headache was gone, but in its place was a jittery sort of exhaustion. She moved around the room picking up a few of the more obvious bits of debris and putting them where they belonged. Dealing with Rafe's things was easier than dealing with him—or her feelings. She hung his coat on a wooden hanger and bit her lip.

She wanted to go home.

With her eyes open, staring at the bright miscellany of his apartment, she could see *her* place, her things—the blue sofa she'd bought secondhand. The crystal lamp she'd bought new, for a ruinous price. Her own pocket-size kitchen, less than half the size of Rafe's, with her baking equipment and cookbook collection.

She was homesick. Oh, my. She shook her head. At twenty-six years old, after living on her own since she was seventeen, she was seriously homesick. How ridiculous. Absently she rubbed her chest, where the ache seemed the strongest, and drifted over to look at the big painting of a jester.

It made her smile. There was that huge, absurd hat, rakishly tilted. The balls that floated so improbably, kept airborne by will or magic. The jester's wicked eyes and cocky grin. He was very sure of himself, certain he could keep all those balls spinning.

"What's the Mona Lisa smile for?"

She turned. Rafe stood at the foot of the stairs, rubbing a towel over his hair. He was wearing silky blue pajama bottoms...and nothing else. Her heartbeat went silly. To compensate, she lifted one eyebrow and answered in her coolest voice. "Have you decided to speak, then?"

He didn't smile. "Sorry. I've been thinking."

"And it's so difficult to do two things at once. Like think and speak."

He brought the towel down across his chest as if chasing a stray drop of water. Her gaze was dragged right along with that towel. "I did irritate you, didn't I?"

"Yes." Was he doing that thing with the towel on purpose? She turned back to the painting. "I like this. Is it from a local gallery?"

"Not a gallery, but it is by a local artist. Maggie painted it for me when I got this place. She claims he reminds her of me."

Oh, that cocky, confident grin... "I'd say she knows you pretty well."

"We seldom know people as well as we'd like to think." His voice told her he'd moved closer. "Why did you do it, Charlie? Why did you sell out my father?"

Her stomach muscles jerked, drawing her spine straight. Her mind filled with the noisy buzz of excuses, explanations, apologies…guilt. She couldn't get a single word out of her dry mouth.

"How much did they pay you? Or was it blackmail—do they have some hold over you? Dammit, Charlie!" His hand closed around her arm, and he turned her to face him. "You owe me some kind of explanation!"

"Maybe I owe your father an explanation. He…" Her voice faltered. She hadn't seen Grant since she'd confessed to the police. She didn't want to see him, but at some point she would have to. Apologies mended nothing and explanations were kissing cousins to excuses, but he deserved at least that much from her. That, and a chance to tell her what he thought of her.

She straightened her shoulders. "But I don't owe you a thing."

"We can't start a marriage with this between us."

She knocked his hand away. "What marriage? Read my lips, Rafe— I am not marrying you."

His upper lip lifted in a snarl of temper. He grabbed her shoulders and crushed his mouth down on hers.

She jolted and tried to shove him away. Quick as a striking snake, he captured her hands and twisted them behind her, holding them easily with one hand while his other grabbed her jaw, trapping her face so she couldn't twist away from his mouth.

It was nothing like the first time he'd kissed her. Then he'd cupped her face in one hand, not captured it in a grip she couldn't break. Then his mouth had been sure and gentle, not hard and hot with demands she couldn't refuse. Her eyes went wide in shock. She couldn't move, couldn't even turn her head aside, could only stand there and let him take her mouth. Fear skittered through her system like fire chasing dried leaves.

But fear was supposed to be cold. This wasn't. The wild current flickering over her skin brought heat, a prickly flush that woke an ache deep inside. He wasn't hurting her. His mouth was eating at hers, and his hand had left her face to caress her throat, his thumb making slow circles over her racing pulse. Her inner thighs clenched. The muscles across her shoulders and back went loose, and her hands were suddenly limp in his grasp.

She'd been wrong. It was exactly like the first time he'd kissed her. Perfect.

Her mouth opened and she knew him, knew his taste and the wild beating of his heart. Her own heartbeat turned strange and unpredictable, a foreign drum sounding a rhythm she didn't understand. A mad confusion seized her, making her want to lick her way down his chest where she could take his heartbeat into her mouth. Making her want to hit him, hurt him, spurn him—or take him deep inside her, so far inside he could never get free again.

It was that confusion rather than any gram of common sense that had her twisting free.

He still held one of her hands. He'd turned loose of the other at some point. She hadn't even noticed. His eyes were dark and hot. "Charlie," he said, and reached for her again.

She flinched.

He froze. Then, moving very slowly, he put his hand on her cheek, just rested it there, his fingers curving up around her temple. "If you were thinking of sticking me with a knife, don't bother. The way you looked just now..." He drew in a shaky breath. "I'm sorry."

"I don't *like* not having a choice." Her voice shook. She hated it. Maybe she hated him, too—for the gentle way he touched her now as much as for the way he'd kissed her a moment ago. "You don't have any right to hold me and—and do those things. No right. You—you— I never know what you're going to do!"

"I didn't know I was going to do that, either." His thumb made a soothing circle on her cheek. "With you, I keep surprising myself."

His tenderness frightened her more than his force had. She tried to make herself move away from that soothing hand. And couldn't.

"What do you want, Charlie? Do you want me to say I'm sorry I hurt you?" His thumb dipped to her mouth, touching the upper lip. "I am."

She stiffened and stepped back. "You didn't hurt me. You made me furious, but you did not hurt me."

One corner of his mouth tucked down in mild frustration. "Whatever you say."

"You're making me furious now, too."

"I make you feel plenty of things, which is why you're angry. We'll have a lively marriage."

Her breath puffed out in exasperation. "Rafe. Be reasonable. Fifty years ago a pregnant single woman might have had to get married for the sake of the baby. That isn't necessary anymore."

"Maybe not necessary, but it's best. Be reasonable," he echoed her, lightly mocking. "I wouldn't make a bad husband. I've got money—and that matters, you know. Maybe more than it should, but the way this world is set up, money can make a big difference in the kind of start a kid gets. It makes a difference in the stress levels of the kid's parents, too. I know you like pretty things, and no one likes worrying about how they're going to pay the bills. I can take good care of you and the baby."

Her mouth tightened. "Thank you very much, but I don't need to be taken care of."

"Then there's family. I've got plenty of that, God knows. I'll admit they can be aggravating at times, but it's good for a kid to have family—aunts, uncles, cousins. Grandparents."

That went right to her gut. A large family was the one thing she couldn't give her child. "Your parents... I think Grant and Emma will accept the baby whether we get married or not."

He grimaced. "Of course they will. When I told them it was my baby you were carrying—"

"You told them? What..." She wanted to know what

they'd said, how they'd reacted. She was afraid she wouldn't like the answer. "When did you tell them?"

"As soon as I got back. I told them I was going to marry you, too."

"I'm sure they loved hearing *that*. Especially your father."

"He didn't object. Look, Charlie, our baby will be a Connelly no matter what its last name is. But if we're not married, *you* won't be part of the family. How do you think our child will feel, knowing that his mother isn't one of the clan? A little different from the rest? Maybe not quite as good?"

She looked away. "Lots of children have divorced parents. They don't all feel like outsiders."

He must have known he was getting to her. He cupped her shoulders. "But we don't have to take the risk that our child will feel that way."

"Talk about risks! Marriage is a risk under the best circumstances. These are hardly the best."

"Everything in life is a risk. If we don't get married, we'll be guaranteeing that our child won't grow up with two parents in the same home." He squeezed her shoulders gently. "What can I say to convince you? Tell me what you want. If it's money—" He paused, grimaced. "We can handle things that way if you like. A settlement of some kind. I've got enough to be generous."

Oh, thank you, she thought, dizzy and numb from the sudden blow. *Thank you for reminding me what you really think about me. What else could I possibly want, but money?*

"So." His smile was a masterpiece—charm with a whiff of seduction from the lingering heat in his eyes. "What do you say?"

She gathered the ragged edges of her pride around her. "I'd say you're a fool to want to marry a woman who's more interested in what you own than what you are." His hands and the skin around his eyes tightened. Good. Her own blow had landed. She smiled at him, bright and brittle. "But that's your affair. I'll give your proposal some thought and get back to you once I decide exactly what it's worth to me."

Nothing, she thought as she turned away. His proposal wasn't worth one damned thing.

This time he didn't try to draw her back. He let her climb the stairs to his bedroom without saying another word.

Rafe swung gently to and fro in the hammock, staring out the undraped window. Night changed the tempo of the city's pulse without altering its restless rhythm. Cars growled, revved, raced, paused and cruised. Lights blinked on in some windows while others winked off. Somewhere a siren howled, muffled by walls and distance.

Here was home. Rafe enjoyed travel; he liked seeing new places, trying new things. The green of a wandering country lane, the rush and rapture of the ocean, the majesty of mountains and the silence of desert—all had a place in his heart, but none were at the center of it the way Chicago was. After a trip for business or pleasure he always settled into the sights, sounds and scents of this city like a child snuggling into his own familiar bed.

Tonight the city held no comfort for him.

All his life Rafe had seen dollar signs in people's eyes when they looked at him. It was an inescapable part of being a Connelly. Even basically decent people were sometimes more conscious of his family's wealth than they were of anything else about him.

He'd been eight when he first realized that some people disliked him simply because his father had money. He'd been as indignant as only an eight-year-old can be. His father had told him that most people had to deal with something along those lines. Whether you were black or freckled, fat or skinny, had a rich father or a funny name—whatever was different, that was what people noticed first. Most of them got past it if you gave them a chance.

On the whole he'd found that to be true. But it was also true that some women never saw beyond what his wealth might bring them, if only he could be persuaded to share some of it. Or all of it, along with his name.

The funny thing was, it had never occurred to him that Charlie might be one of those women. Not until she'd jumped to the conclusion that he was trying to buy her. Now that she'd put the idea in his head, he couldn't get rid of it.

You're a fool to want to marry a woman who's more interested in what you own than what you are.

Was that the most important fact about him to Charlie? What he owned?

When he'd offered a settlement, he'd been thinking about the power that money confers. Earlier she'd asked him if he would try to take custody of their child away from her if she didn't marry him. That had smarted, but after thinking it over, he could see that she might feel powerless. He'd thought to reassure her by giving her money of her own, money he didn't control. Instead he'd made her furious...and made himself doubt.

Charlie didn't know how to fight, though. She held tight to her temper the way she held on to all her emotions, as if relaxing her grip might leave some stray feeling out where people could see it and use it against her.

She needed to surprise herself more.

Well, he could help her with that. God knew he surprised himself with her. It was only fair if she was off-balance with him, too. And it would be good for her to loosen some of that too-tight control she put on herself.

She hadn't been controlled in bed. She hadn't been thinking about his money then, either. She'd burned for him, dammit. He wasn't wrong about that. Charlie might keep her emotions under lock and key most of the time, but when she let them out they were as real and honest as a thunderstorm.

He'd screwed up. Big-time.

Rafe scowled and shifted, making the hammock rock. The fact was, she'd scared him. He hadn't liked that, hadn't wanted to admit she had that much power over him, so he'd stayed away. He'd done his damnedest to shut her out of his mind, secretly glad for the business trip that took him out of Chicago for the next few months.

He knew how women felt about men who don't call. It was high on their list of Unforgivable Male Sins. Whatever Charlie said now, he had hurt her.

Calling her a month later didn't count, he admitted. That had been a matter of pride and conscience. He'd known there was a chance their lovemaking could have resulted in complications, and his own good opinion of himself hadn't let him duck that responsibility.

Maybe he'd wanted to talk to her again, too. Maybe he'd wanted that every bit as much as he'd wanted to stay away from her, and maybe it had hurt when she didn't return his call. Not a lot, he assured himself. But it had hurt a little bit.

He put his hand against the wall and gave a push, setting the hammock to swinging again. Things were majorly complicated, all right. He'd hurt her. She'd betrayed his father. What kind of marriage could they have when they didn't trust each other? When they each had good reason not to trust?

At the back of his mind he'd always thought that if he ever *did* get married, he would want what his parents had— something real and solid. They'd hit some rough patches, but they'd come out stronger in the end. Not many people had what they did. Too often marriage made people mean or crazy or unhappy. He supposed that had been another reason he'd steered clear of it. He hadn't wanted to marry unless he could do it right. He hadn't wanted to try for that and fail.

His mouth thinned. He hadn't failed yet. Hell, he hadn't managed to talk her into marriage yet. One thing at a time, he told himself. She'd wanted him once. He was pretty sure she still did, so he had that on his side. God knew he wanted her, too. Sometimes he wasn't sure which he wanted more—to shake her or kiss her—but even when the shaking sounded really appealing, he still wanted to kiss her.

Charlie would end up in his bed. That much he promised himself. The trust business, though... He sighed. That was going to take a lot more thought.

It would be a helluva lot easier to trust her if she'd just tell him what was going on. If he knew *why* she'd done what she had... When you got right down to it, he didn't know much about her. He wouldn't even have known her parents were dead if it hadn't been in her personnel file at Connelly Corporation.

Oh, he knew one or two of her secrets now. He brooded over that as the hammock rocked gently. He'd had to do some digging to find her, and wouldn't she be mad if she knew that? She'd had some rough times as a kid, Charlie had. But dammit, she didn't have to make a big secret out of everything.

It would be easy to learn more. Between him and Dix, there wasn't much that couldn't be pried out of various records, including the ones at the police department. But he knew what her reaction would be if she found out he'd gone behind her back that way. You don't go about building trust by hacking into a person's past.

Hell. He was going to have to do this the hard way, wasn't he?

Five

In another part of Chicago, in a twelfth-floor room at a large hotel, Edwin Tefteller held a cellular phone to his ear. The drapes were drawn. The radio, tuned to a classical station, played just loudly enough to muffle any sounds of the city that might leak in through the walls.

He was a smallish man, only five foot six, but trim and very erect. His face was soft, clean, round. The skin was firm enough to suggest that his receding hairline had arrived prematurely. The neat little mustache beneath his nose was sandy brown, like the thinning hair on his head. His white dress shirt was of decent quality and moderate price, like his dark shoes and slacks and the conservatively striped tie knotted at his throat. The one small note of vanity or extravagance was sounded by his glasses, which had a designer frame. The lenses were clear glass, but no one could tell that by looking.

All in all, he looked like a man who ate his vegetables, flossed after meals and paid his bills on time, a man who could sail through an IRS audit without breaking a sweat. And he was. Most people looked at him and thought "accountant."

They were wrong.

Edwin's index finger tapped the little cell phone with restrained impatience. At last a voice came on the other end. "This had better be important. It's after one-thirty in the morning. My wife gives me hell when the phone wakes her up."

"I do not make a habit of calling about trivial matters," Edwin said. "You have violated our agreement."

"I don't know what you're talking about."

Edwin sighed. Employers preferred to consider him a tool. On the whole, it was convenient to allow them to think of him this way. Had they realized how much of their affairs he knew or inferred, it would have made them uneasy. But while Edwin might permit employers to underestimate him, he did not allow them to take him for a fool. "I have an exclusive contract with you, Mr. Kelly. I work alone. Always. I believe I made that clear at the outset."

"I'm aware of the terms of our agreement," Jimmie Kelly growled. "Especially the godawful amount of up-front money you demanded."

"I am relieved to hear it. Perhaps you can explain why the same bumbler who botched the first attempt was allowed to interfere in *my* contract, then."

"I still don't know what you're talking about. And Palermo's no bungler."

"He failed to kill the Masters woman once. That is why you contacted me, isn't it?" Edwin let a small silence fall. There was a great deal more to the situation than that, but it wouldn't pay to advertise his knowledge at this point. "That, and you appreciated the dispatch with which I took care of the earlier job with the private investigator. I, in turn, appreciated the dispatch with which you paid my fee. I am disappointed by your disregard of our agreement this time, however. I will not tolerate sharing a contract with others.''

''I told you I'd pull Palermo off the Masters job. If my word isn't good enough—''

''Today at 4:43 p.m., Rocky Palermo tried to run down Charlotte Masters with a '98 Buick—stolen, I assume. If your chief enforcer was not acting on your orders, you have a disciplinary problem.''

There was a tiny, betraying pause before Kelly exploded. ''Damn right there's a problem! He's supposed to be keeping track of her for you, not trying to take her out. I'll straighten him out.''

''You do that,'' Edwin murmured. Palermo had, of course, acted on orders. The Kellys' chief enforcer wasn't in Edwin's class, but neither was he stupid. No doubt Jimmie Kelly thought he could refuse to pay the other half of Edwin's fee if his own man made the hit. It was a mistaken assumption, but in some ways Kelly was a simple man.

''I was prepared to complete the job tomorrow night, quietly and without fuss. Your man's blundering attempt alerted her that her whereabouts were known. Naturally, she has disappeared. I stand to lose a great deal of time tracking her down a second time. I cannot and will not tolerate having my contract interfered with again.''

''Dammit to hell, I've told you I'd take care of it.''

''You will understand, I'm sure, that I must refuse to share my information with you now. I would hate to have to eliminate Mr. Palermo, but if he were to interfere again, I would be forced to.''

The silence was longer this time. ''I want to be kept informed.''

''I will let you know when I am prepared to complete the job. I will not tell you where the target is.'' Kelly hadn't found the woman. Edwin had. He saw no point in tempting his employer into misbehavior again.

Kelly needed to assert his authority with trivial demands and veiled threats. Edwin allowed him that. Employers

wished to feel they controlled their tool. And they did, as
long as they dealt with him according to the terms of their
agreement.

After the call ended, Edwin put the cell phone back in
his briefcase. Kelly had dealt with him squarely the first
time, when he had killed the detective. Now, however, he
was trying to save a few dollars. Edwin's mouth curved in
dry humor as he carefully unknotted his tie. It was amazing,
really, what avarice would tempt people into. One wouldn't
think that one of the top killers in the world would have to
worry about being cheated, but now and then a client considered himself so powerful that he could rewrite their deal
after a job was completed.

Edwin did not kill clients, even when they were difficult.
It would be bad for business. Instead he acquired information. In this instance it shouldn't be difficult to ensure
that the Kellys dealt with him properly. One phone call to
the police or to Grant Connelly would cost them a great
deal more money than they owed Edwin.

He unbuttoned the top button of his shirt and hung up
the tie, then took a file folder from his briefcase and sat at
the table. The folder held a neat sheaf of papers with a
color photograph on top—a woman's face, unsmiling. He
picked it up.

Charlotte Masters was wearing a high-necked blouse—
tasteful and modest, Edwin thought. Her hair was smooth,
unfussy; though the color was a bit showy, it was her nat-
ural color, so Edwin didn't hold that against her. She was
tidy, a trait he esteemed. He'd learned that while investigating the apartment she'd abandoned after Palermo
botched the first hit.

Edwin's mouth pursed in distaste. Amateurs annoyed
him. Palermo was a professional criminal, but having killed
in the course of his duties did not make him a professional
killer. He was certainly not a marksman. Hubris or envy of
his betters had led him to attempt a shot few professionals
would have tried. He deserved to have failed.

He set the photo down and studied the next paper in the pile, a floor plan of Charlotte Master's old apartment. One could learn a great deal about a target's habits from the way they arranged their living space. Additionally, of course, he had acquired details from investigating her belongings that had helped establish her habits, preferences, possible contacts. Some of the papers in the folder had come from the orderly files in her desk.

She was efficient, honest, responsible—altogether an admirable woman. Of course, she did have a weakness. Her brother. Brad Masters had been a burden on his older sister ever since their parents' deaths. He had provided the lever the Kellys had used to coerce her into betraying her employer.

But few people possessed the strength to completely sever outside ties the way Edwin had done. All in all, she was a worthy quarry.

There was a knock on the door. As matter-of-factly as another man might save an open file on the computer before responding to an interruption, he put the file away and removed a small, snub-nosed gun from the briefcase. He was expecting room service, having ordered his dinner earlier. But he assumed nothing. After covering the gun with a hotel towel, he moved to the door. "Yes?" he said pleasantly.

When the voice on the other side of the door confirmed that it belonged to room service, he arranged the towel so that it looked as if he'd been drying his hands, and opened the door. The waiter remained cheerfully unaware that a gun was trained on him the entire time he was in the room. He left with an adequate, if not generous, tip, and Edwin sat down to his meal—a salad with the dressing on the side, broiled salmon, and a baked potato, dry.

Forty minutes later, the tray holding his dishes sat outside the door and the folder was open once more. He had several possibilities for locating his target, but the most certain was the way he had found her the first time: the brother. Eventually she would contact him.

He lingered over her photograph. A pretty woman. Edwin appreciated beauty, but didn't admire it. No, it was her other qualities he esteemed. She deserved him, he thought. Not an amateur like Palermo. Suffering was messy, the mark of a poorly executed job.

Unlike Palermo, he was an excellent marksman. A bullet in the brain would assure that the admirable Ms. Masters didn't suffer. She would be dead before she realized what had happened.

Six

Charlotte scrunched her head deeper into the pillow, reluctant to leave her dream behind. But it was drifting away already...something about a project at the office, an important project she had to finish....

The office, she thought fuzzily. Was it time to get up? If so, her alarm would tell her soon. She always set the alarm. Not once had she been late since she started working for Grant.

Her eyes flew open. No office. No job working for Grant Connelly. No job at all, she realized as her sleepy brain caught up with memory. She stared up at the ceiling, and it was the wrong ceiling. Not the one above her own bed in her apartment—because that, too, was gone.

Everything. Everything she'd worked so hard for was gone.

She flung the covers back and threw herself out of bed, blinking furiously. She would *not* give in to self-pity.

The light streaming in the wide, high window in Rafe's

bedroom told her she'd slept late. She glanced at the clock and grimaced. It was nearly ten. Normally she was a morning person, but she'd had to adapt her schedule to work at Hole-in-the-Wall.

She had to get back there. Today. She needed her backpack. She needed her money, too. Rafe had dragged her out last night with a total of twenty-two dollars and thirty cents in tips in her pocket.

Fourteen minutes later she'd done what she could to make herself presentable—pretty much a lost cause with no makeup, blow-dryer or clean clothes. She settled for wearing yesterday's skirt with another of Rafe's sweatshirts and headed downstairs, prepared for an argument.

He wasn't there.

Well. She put her hands on her hips. This was convenient, she told herself, not annoying. Rafe certainly didn't need to let her know what he was doing every minute, and she didn't need an argument. She poured herself a glass of milk and sat down at the table with the telephone directory.

Rafe slammed into his apartment over an hour after leaving it, sweatier but no more relaxed than when he'd left. Usually a good run cleared his mind. Not today.

Nothing worked the way it was supposed to with Charlie around, he thought in disgust, pulling off his sweatshirt as he headed upstairs for a shower. The T-shirt he'd worn beneath it was damp. He'd pushed himself pretty hard at the park, for all the good it had done him. He was no closer to getting a grip on the trust thing than he had been last night.

Maybe a hot shower would—wait a minute. The door to his bedroom door was open. Charlie must be awake at last.

The least he could do was share his frustration with her, he decided.

He stopped in the doorway. His bed was made. The sweats he'd loaned her were folded and placed neatly in the middle of the bed. Charlie was nowhere in sight.

He raced back to the stairs. "Charlie!" he bellowed. "Dammit, you'd better be here!"

She wasn't. His heart was pounding harder than it had during his run by the time he finished a hasty, pointless search of the apartment. Keep calm, he told himself. There were no signs that she'd been forced to leave, no indications of a struggle. Or violence.

Had she left because of the kiss he'd forced on her last night? Had he scared her that badly—or made her too mad to think straight? But she didn't have anywhere to go, or any money to get there.

Unless she'd taken some of his.

He dashed back upstairs. His wallet was right where he'd left it last night—on the bathroom floor next to his pants. He didn't bother to look in it. Charlie might be able to persuade herself she was justified in borrowing money from him, but she would never have put the wallet back on the floor after rifling it.

No money, no car, no clothes besides what she wore on her back—and with a hit man looking for her. "Dammit, Charlie," he muttered, his fists tight at his sides. "Where are you?"

Charlotte pushed the buzzer and waited, her foot tapping. She just hoped Rafe was back from wherever he'd gone earlier. She didn't fancy waiting around in the tiny foyer while he ran his mysterious errands. The other people in the building were likely to call the police if she hung around too long.

She shoved the sleeves of his leather coat back up—they kept slipping down and swallowing her hands—and shifted her backpack to the other shoulder. He was just going to have to trust her with a key. He'd forced her to come here, after all, so the least—

"Yes?" came a tinny voice from the intercom.

"It's Charlie. I—"

"Stay there!"

"Rafe?"

No answer. She stared at the intercom. Now what?

Moments later she heard feet thundering down the stairs. Alarm quickened her heartbeat. Whatever had upset Rafe must be urgent if he hadn't wanted to wait for an elevator. His apartment was on the fifth floor.

The door to the service stairs crashed open and he burst out of it at a dead run. "For God's sake, where have you been?" He grabbed her shoulders.

"What's wrong? What's happened?"

"You take off without a word and you ask me what's wrong?"

She frowned. "You're yelling."

"Damned right I'm yelling! You go off without leaving a note, without making any effort to let me know if you've been abducted or killed—"

"I'll be sure to leave you a note if I'm killed or kidnapped. Look, you're digging holes in my shoulders. And *you* didn't leave *me* a note when you left the apartment."

"I don't have a hit man trying to kill me!" He was still much too loud, but his fingers stopped playing hole-puncher. "Dammit, Charlie—"

The elevator doors opened. A skinny woman with blue hair and a large rat on a leash—well, it was probably a dog, but it looked like a rat—stood in the elevator. She gave Rafe a dubious glance.

He switched his grip to Charlotte's hand and dragged her into the elevator, glaring at the woman. She and her rat stepped out quickly.

As soon as the elevator doors closed, Rafe dropped her hand. They rode up in stiff silence. On Rafe's part the silence might have been generated by anger. For Charlotte it came from sheer bewilderment.

He'd yelled at her. He was furious. He'd raced down those stairs as if he'd been frantic about her. She didn't understand. A man who climbed out of a woman's bed without a backward glance didn't go ballistic with worry just because she didn't leave him a note. Even given her current circumstances, his reaction didn't make sense.

A small motion inside her womb gave her the answer. She touched her stomach. Of course. Rafe had been worried about the baby, not her. He was serious about wanting this child. The thought should have reassured her. Instead her spirits sank. *Oh, no,* she thought, her eyes closing. *It can't matter. I couldn't be such a fool....*

The elevator doors opened. He grabbed her arm. She jerked it away and glared at him. "Quit dragging me around like a suitcase!"

"If you were a suitcase you'd stay where I put you." He headed for his door. "Come on, or I'll reach for your handle again."

She huffed out an exasperated breath and followed him. "Your courting technique lacks a certain something."

He yanked his door open and stormed inside. "I've got it in mind to be a husband, not a widower! What the hell were you thinking of? What could possibly be important enough to risk your life for?"

"This." She swung her backpack off her shoulder. "And I didn't risk my life. I called Nikki—"

"Your backpack?" He glared at the innocuous canvas tote. "*That's* what you were so desperate to get?"

"Everything I own is in that! My money, my ID, my—"

"You want money?" He dug out his wallet, pulled out a wad of bills—and threw them at her. "Here! You've got money now!"

Bills flew everywhere. Some fluttered to the floor at her feet. One landed on his shoe. Others scattered randomly on the floor between them, expensive green and white confetti. She stood frozen, staring at him, unable to believe he'd just thrown the entire contents of his wallet at her.

He scowled back at her.

Slowly she stepped forward. She unzipped her backpack and knelt in front of him, shoving the dratted sleeves of his coat up again. Then she began to empty out the contents, one by one.

"*This* is what was so important." She pulled out her mother's copy of *Little Women*. "I needed the money, yes." Other books followed—her high school yearbook, her address book, an old photo album, a very old volume of Mother Goose stories that her grandmother had read to her mother. "Believe it or not, rich man, it's hard to get by in this world without money."

She paused to stroke the jeweler's box she pulled out next. Most of the velvet had worn off. Inside were her mother's wedding ring, her father's watch and the tiny diamond earrings she'd bought with her first paycheck from Connelly Corporation. "But I needed these things more than the money."

Tilting the backpack, she emptied out the rest of her possessions—which included a hairbrush, toothbrush, toothpaste and shampoo. Extra pairs of panties and socks. A few more mementos, including the fancy gold-plated fountain pen Grant had given her for Christmas last year. Last she pulled out the things in the outside pocket: her birth certificate and the envelope containing all that was left of her savings; two hundred thirteen dollars.

She sat back on her heels and stared up at him, stony faced. "That's everything I own in this world now. And yes, it would have been worth risking my life to get these things back, but I didn't. I called a woman who works at Hole-in-the-Wall and asked her to bring my things to me. We met at the Irving Park El station so she wouldn't know where I'm staying."

Rafe was looking down at the small pile of objects at his feet with a sort of horrified fascination. He grimaced, scrubbed a hand over his face and met her eyes. "Why didn't you tell me why you needed your backpack?"

After the way he'd acted when she tried to get him to go back for it? She shook her head in disbelief. "Why? What good would it have done?"

He sighed, knelt and began gathering her treasures, slipping them into the backpack with more care than she'd thought he possessed. "Next time tell me if you need to go somewhere," he said quietly. "Don't go off alone. I don't want you risking yourself that way. If I can't go with you, I'll get someone else to. Hey." His hands paused. A grin spread over his face. "I gave you this."

He held up the tacky souvenir he'd brought her from Hawaii last year—a plastic hula dancer with bare bumps for breasts and a grass skirt that had been shedding steadily for months.

Her face heated. "I keep it to remind me of you," she said, snatching it out of his hand and stuffing it in the backpack. "Lewd, crude and obvious."

He was still grinning, damn him. "You like me."

She rolled her eyes and tucked *Little Women* back where it belonged.

"You may be mad at me, but you like me. If you didn't, you wouldn't…"

When he didn't finish the sentence she glanced up. This time he held a packet of letters tied by a blue ribbon, a slight frown on his face.

She grabbed the letters away, too. "Have you no sense of private property? Those are personal."

"You shouldn't put things at my feet if you don't want me to see them." But he helped her pick up the rest of her things without further comment, then sat back on his heels. "Ah, about the money I threw at you…"

She raised both eyebrows. "What about it?"

"That was childish of me."

"I agree."

"Yes. Well…" He pushed to his feet, glanced at the door—which still stood open—made an exasperated sound and stalked over to close and lock it. Then he started to pace.

Her eyes followed him. He was wearing a pair of jeans so old they were white in interesting places and a dark blue

turtleneck with a frayed hem. He looked more like an un-
employed stuntman than an heir to one of Chicago's biggest fortunes.

He looked delicious. She swallowed, shoved up a sleeve
and zipped the backpack.

"The thing is," he said, stopping abruptly, "I don't want
you to think... That is, after what I said last night you
might—I didn't throw money at you because I was trying
to buy you, dammit!"

"I know that. You're an idiot, but not that much of an
idiot."

His mouth stretched in a thin, exasperated line. "How
do you do that?"

"What?"

"I'm standing, you're on the floor, and you still manage
to look down your nose at me."

"It's a gift." She stood and took off the too-big coat,
draping it over her arm. "Since you don't want me to go
out by myself, perhaps you'd like to go shopping. Your
sweats are comfortable, but the fit isn't great."

"We can go shopping, but not today."

"Look, you don't get to have everything your way. I'm
not talking about a major shopping trip—just a few essen-
tials. I can't keep wearing the same clothes every day. And
I need some prenatal vitamins."

"Prenatal vitamins?" He frowned. "Are those some special kind?"

"They have extra nutrients the baby needs."

"Damn. I didn't think of that. Dix will be here later with
some of your things. I told him to be sure to bring all your
shoes— I know women have a thing about shoes. Maybe
you can explain that to me sometime. My sisters sure love
to buy shoes. It's their second-favorite thing, next to choc-
olate. But I didn't think to tell Dix to look for some special
kind of vitamins."

She blinked, trying to keep up with the main point.
"What do you mean, Dix will be here with my things?"

"He's going to stop by your old apartment today. Not the crummy room and a bath that's your most recent old apartment. The one where we…ah, the one you had before."

She knew what he'd almost said: the one where they'd made love. No, he probably thought of it as the place where they'd had sex. Her mouth thinned. "And just how is he going to get in?"

"That shouldn't be a problem." He rubbed his chin. "They have prenatal vitamins at drugstores, don't they? I can have some delivered. Anything else you need right away?"

"I don't think so. Are you just going to leave your money all over the floor?"

"I'm trying to figure out how to give some of it to you without getting it thrown in my face."

Her lips twitched. "I don't throw money around. Offer me a blunt object, though, and see what happens."

He snorted and began gathering the bills. She found herself just standing there watching him. He looked so good to her. *And he isn't even trying. I look at him and I want him. He doesn't even have to do anything.* She wasn't sure if it was him or her own wayward hormones she resented more.

Her mouth tight, she went to hang up his coat.

"What did you tell your friend?" he asked, reaching for the empty billfold he'd dropped on the floor during his little temper fit. "The one who brought you the backpack."

"Nikki saw you drag me out of there last night, so I had to account for your odd behavior. I made up this ridiculous story about two boyfriends. There's this poor but honest fellow I broke up with before coming to work at Hole-in-the-Wall, and a rich, abusive man I'm hiding from."

"Which one am I?"

"Poor but honest. You have some self-esteem problems," she added. "I left you because your jealousy was driving me crazy. Nikki loved it. Here, you missed a twenty.'' She held it out.

''I don't suppose you... No, I'll have to find some other way.'' After pocketing the twenty he added, ''The bit about the abusive boyfriend. Was that to explain why someone might come around looking for you?''

Her eyebrows went up. ''Very good.''

''I'm not stupid. It won't be enough for your friend to keep quiet, you know. Too many others saw me at Hole-in-the-Wall.''

''That's why I also told her you were taking me back to Jamestown, New York. That's your hometown, you see. With the best intentions in the world, Nikki is incapable of keeping a secret. She'll tell one or two people in confidence, and pretty soon the story of our romantic elopement will be common knowledge at Hole-in-the-Wall. If anyone does come looking for me there, he'll think I've left the city.''

He nodded thoughtfully. ''That may help. I've another bit of misdirection in mind, too. I thought it might be best if people think your baby is...well, if they think my father is responsible.''

She sputtered. ''No way. Absolutely, positively no way.''

''The Kellys know you're pregnant. It's only logical for them to keep an eye on the father of your baby in order to find you. I don't want them looking for you here, and my father...well, you *were* his secretary.''

''Executive assistant,'' she said coldly.

''Whatever. The point is, people are likely to believe the story. He, uh, has something of a history.''

She knew what he meant. In addition to the twin sons, now grown, who had so recently come forward to join the family, there was Seth. Seth Connelly had been raised by Grant and Emma from the age of twelve, but he wasn't Emma's son. Many years ago Grant had had an affair with his secretary. Gossip said that he and Emma had been separated at the time of the affair, the marriage in trouble, but somehow it had survived.

The secretary's name was Angie Donahue. After handing over custody of her son eighteen years ago she'd left without a backward glance...until recently. She was also the niece of the head of the Kellys' family-run criminal organization, and the daughter of another of the bosses.

Charlotte wished with all her heart Angie had stayed out of sight. "Rafe, that was years and years ago. I promise you, your father has never been anything but professional and respectful in his dealings with me."

He gave her an exasperated look. "I know that. But the Kellys don't. And, given Angie's connection to them—well, they'll probably buy it. Maybe it will keep them looking in all the wrong places."

"But your mother...it's not worth it."

"Look, I wasn't asking for your vote. I've already called my mother this morning, and—"

"You didn't!" She stared at him in horror.

"And my grandmother." He grimaced. "Now there's a sacrifice. Talk about being put through the third degree! She'll know exactly how to go about things, though. She plans to deny everything. According to her, that will get the gossips buzzing, but the story won't really stick. After we're married everyone will agree they never believed a word of it. If—"

The buzzer sounded.

"Damn. Hold on a minute." Rafe went to the intercom and pushed the button. She couldn't hear what the other person said, but Rafe's response was clear enough, if puzzling. "She turned up...yeah, that's what I thought, too. Come on up." He punched the off button.

"Tell me that's not your mother, coming to strangle me."

"You're in luck. That was Lucas Starwind."

"The detective your father hired?"

He nodded. "When you pulled your disappearing act this

morning, I called Luke to help me find you. He was supposed to come over later today anyway. We've been working together on some things.''

"What sort of things?"

"We're both trying to find out what the Kellys are up to, though we're coming at it from different angles."

"Oh, you're trying to find out what the tech from Broderton's Computing did, aren't you?" Eager, she took a few steps closer. "I went into the office on weekends, but couldn't figure out what he'd done to the system. Have you made any progress?"

He gave her a funny look. "Some."

His expression stopped her short. "I wanted to undo whatever damage I'd caused. Maybe trying doesn't count when I failed. But I did try."

There was a knock at the door. Rafe glanced at it and sighed. "We'll talk later."

He checked through the peephole before opening the door. "Come in. You know Charlie already, don't you?"

"We've met." The man who entered was tall—about Rafe's height, maybe a little more. His hair and eyes were dark. So was his expression. She'd met Luke Starwind twice when he'd come to the office to give Grant a report. She hadn't liked him much. He was too controlled, too distant...*too much like me,* she thought, and her mouth turned down.

He gave her a cool, appraising glance. "Ms. Masters. You've been hard to find. For an amateur, you're pretty good at vanishing."

"Not good enough, apparently. Can I get you something to drink, or shall we go straight to the interrogation?"

"Coffee would be good." He turned to Rafe, dismissing her. "Fill me in. How did you find her?"

"He didn't find me," Charlotte said, irritated at being spoken of as if she weren't there. "I made it back here all by myself, without so much as a pair of handcuffs as motivation."

"I meant how did he find you yesterday, not this morning. I take my coffee black," he added pointedly.

She had her mouth open, ready to offer a polite suggestion about what he could do with the coffeepot, when Rafe's hand landed on her shoulder.

"Whoa, champ." He slid an amused glance from her to the detective. "Much as I'd enjoy watching the two of you go a few rounds, we've got a lot of territory to cover today. I'll make the coffee."

Seven

Charlie put the coffee on.

Rafe shook his head. He should have known that as soon as he said he'd do it, she'd be bound and determined to take over.

"Sorry," Luke said in a low voice while Charlie was in the kitchen. "I shouldn't have made that crack about coffee. She's got quite a mouth when she's irritated, doesn't she?"

"Charlie bristles up like a porcupine if you put her on the defensive. Before I start, do you have any news?"

"Nothing worth mentioning. Are you ready to—" He glanced at the kitchen. "Never mind. You can fill me in on your progress later."

Rafe grimaced. He wasn't crazy about secrets the way Charlie was, but for now he'd have to keep a few. "Let's sit down."

The two men moved to the area Rafe's sisters insisted on calling the conversation pit, where a couple of chairs faced the couch. He sat with his legs spread and frowned at the empty fireplace, organizing what he needed to tell the P.I.

Pretty much everything, he decided. He wouldn't mention proposing—that was personal. What about the letters in her backpack? Those damned letters she was hanging on to, the ones tied together with a pretty blue bow? Love letters, he supposed, scowling. From some man named Brad Fowler. He'd seen the return address.

Deer Lodge Prison.

Was Brad Fowler the reason Charlie had cooperated with the Kellys? Had she been involved with this crook, and that was the hold they had over her? Dammit, he could find out who the man was easily enough…but he'd decided not to hack into her past.

Some sense made him glance at the kitchen. She was standing in the doorway.

Difficult woman, he thought. Cute as could be in that short skirt and his sweatshirt, but difficult. She was in a snit about something. She didn't say anything, just stood there, her arms crossed, and listened while he brought Luke up to date about the way he'd tracked her down, the car that had almost hit her and her excursion that morning.

Maybe he should have told Luke about the letters, too, but he didn't. He wanted Charlie to tell him about them, dammit. About Brad Fowler.

She vanished briefly about the time Luke started asking questions about Hole-in-the-Wall and whether anyone there would be able to identify Rafe. When she reappeared, she had two mugs of coffee.

"Do you prefer to hear things secondhand, Mr. Starwind?" she asked sweetly as she handed Luke one of the mugs. "Or would you like to ask me some questions, too?"

Oh, so that's what was bugging her. She thought they were playing "boys' club—girls keep out." At least, he hoped that's what she assumed.

This trust business was about to get tricky.

"I've got questions," Luke said. "Are you ready to answer them?"

Her glance darted off Rafe and veered quickly back to Luke. "That depends on what you ask."

"Why do the Kellys want you dead?"

Her hand jerked. She narrowly avoided getting scalded by the hot coffee in the mug she still held. Rafe gave Luke a hard look, stood and took the cup from her. "Come on. Sit down."

She let him steer her to a place on the couch beside him, but she didn't sit very close. Not close enough for him to touch. When she answered Luke's question she was looking at him, not Rafe. "I suppose they want revenge. They shot at me as I was leaving police headquarters, so they must have thought I'd told the police what I knew."

"You're the key witness against Angie Donahue."

"I guess so." She didn't look happy about it. Rafe wasn't happy about it, either.

"Can you identify any of them other than Angie?"

"No. That is, there was just the one man who contacted me. I'd know his voice if I ever heard it again, but I never saw him. Lieutenant Johnson at the Special Investigative Unit said a voice identification wouldn't stand up in court."

"How did this man contact you?"

"I've been through all this with Lieutenant Johnson."

"Someone in the department has put a lid on everything connected to your testimony. All we know is that you used the tech the Kellys told you to use, and that you implicated Angie Donahue."

"I really don't know anything that will help."

"Charlie." Rafe leaned toward her. "You said you'd been going in on weekends, trying to undo what you allowed them to do. You haven't been able to. Help us fix things now."

She met his eyes and nodded jerkily. "All right, though I don't think it will do you any good. The first time they contacted me was back in May. I was on my way home, hurrying because it was dark. There were people around, though, so I wasn't really worried. Until *he* came up behind me." Her fingers twitched, closing on air then opening again. "He told me he had a gun, warned me to keep walking and not turn around. He wanted me to arrange for a particular technician to work on the computers at the office. He said…" She swallowed. "I refused, of course."

"You turned him down?" Rafe asked sharply.

"At first. But when I got back to my apartment…I was going to call the police. I *was*. But he—he'd left something there that changed my mind."

"What?"

She shook her head.

"For God's sake, Charlie. If they have some hold over you, tell us what it is so we can help." *So I'll know whether or not I can trust you.*

"They don't. Not anymore. The police…took care of things."

"We need to know what they used to force your cooperation." Rafe hesitated, then added softly, "*I* need to know."

"They…threatened someone important to me." She looked down at her lap, where her hands were holding tightly to each other. "I can't tell you more than that. I'm sorry, but I can't."

Rafe leaned back, frustrated and disappointed.

Luke took over the questioning. He kept at it for nearly an hour, coming back to the same things over and over, but in the end he admitted she was probably right—she didn't know anything useful. She couldn't provide a link to any of the criminals except Angie Donahue. And Angie wasn't talking.

"There's some good news, anyway, from your point of view," Luke said after emptying his mug for the second time. "Angie's lawyered up. As long as she plays the game by their rules, the Kellys are obliged to support her. Ordinarily they might not go as far as killing off the primary witness against her. In her own right, Angie is small potatoes. But her uncle is the head of the family, and her father has risen pretty high in the organization, too.''

"When do you get to the good news?" she asked dryly.

"They won't try as hard," Rafe said abruptly as things clicked into place. "That's what you mean, isn't it, Luke? There no urgency to silencing Charlie because the bosses aren't personally threatened. They're doing this as a matter of—well, call it family ties. Or good employee relations."

Charlie made a choked sound that might have been a laugh.

"That's one way of putting it." Luke put his empty mug on the table. "If Ms. Masters were able to incriminate one of the top people, they'd make killing her a priority. She'd have to go to a safe house—"

"I am not going to trust my life to the police," Charlie put in quickly. "The Kellys could have informants on the force."

"As things stand, it may be okay for you to stay here for now. The police think Rocky Palermo was responsible for the attempt on your life."

"Who is he?"

"The Kellys' chief enforcer. He takes care of their dirty work. The cops are keeping an eye on him, but that doesn't mean you can be careless. No more solo expeditions like the one this morning. Aside from the danger from the Kellys, there's the little matter of the outstanding warrant for your arrest."

All the blood drained from her face. "Oh, God."

"I take it you didn't know."

She shook her head violently. "They—the lieutenant said Grant didn't want charges pressed. He said…" Her voice wobbled and she held her hand to her mouth as if trying to cram the shakes back inside.

"Dammit, Luke! Don't you have some widows and orphans you can go kick? Charlie." Rafe put a hand on her arm. She was stiff, resisting his touch. He ignored that.

"The warrant is just a technicality. It's for being a material witness. They issued it when you vanished."

"The police don't like it when their key witness does a fade." Luke studied Charlie, then shifted his gaze to Rafe. "They don't like it when people harbor someone with a warrant out, either."

"Luke," Rafe growled, "if you don't put a sock in it, I'm going to have to do it for you."

Luke's eyebrows lifted. "I'm not trying to scare her. There's a solution. A good lawyer can go to the cops, get them to drop the charges in exchange for her promise to appear to testify as needed. The police can contact the lawyer when they need her. I can't do it," he added irritably, as if Rafe had asked him to. "A lawyer can act for her without getting in trouble for not revealing her whereabouts."

She'd gotten some color back. "I don't have money for a lawyer."

"I do," Rafe said. He ran his hand down her arm to her hand, closing his fingers around hers. "No arguments this time, Charlie."

She looked down at their joined hands and swallowed. "I'll pay you back."

"No, you won't. It's an investment. I don't want my kid going to jail before he's born."

"Since you put it that way..." She looked up. "Okay. We'll do it your way this time. Just don't think of this as the start of a trend."

"Heaven forbid." Relieved, he grinned at her.

The buzzer sounded again, and relief leaked right back out of him. *Great timing, Dix.*

"You expecting anyone?" Luke asked.

"Dix," Rafe said without looking away from Charlie. They were about to hit the sticky part, and he still didn't have a clue how to handle it. "You want to buzz him up for me, Luke?"

The P.I. hesitated a second, then stood. "Sure."

A frown was tugging at Charlie's mouth. "Dix is the friend of yours that helped you find me, isn't he? The hacker."

"Ah, look, Charlie..." He dropped her hand to run his through his hair. "Damn. I can't come up with a good way to do this. I have to ask you to wait down here while we're working. We'll be in my office."

At first she didn't get it. He could tell because she just looked puzzled, then annoyed.

Then all the expression drained out of her face. "Oh. Of course. You're working on the problem with the corporation's computers, and your hacker friend is helping you." She used both hands to smooth her skirt—though from what Rafe could see, there wasn't enough of it to wrinkle—and stood. "I'll go practice my knitting while you men are busy."

Her voice was so polite, her shoulders so straight, her smile so small and brittle. She was breaking his heart. "If it was just me," he began, rising. "If there weren't so many others involved—"

"I quite understand. Naturally you couldn't let me be privy to what you're doing. I'm responsible for the problem."

"No, dammit, you're not. The Kellys are responsible. You're—"

"An accomplice. Though your father was kind enough not to want me prosecuted for it."

Luke turned away from the intercom. "He's on his way up." He glanced from Rafe to Charlie. "Is there a problem?"

"Not at all," she said.

"Yes," Rafe said at the same time. "I mean no. Charlie will be working with us today."

Luke's expression didn't change. After a moment he said, "That could be a problem, all right."

* * *

She was getting used to him calling her Charlie. Maybe she was starting to like it.

"You have two big computers *and* a laptop?" She shook her head. "Men and their techno-toys."

Charlotte was sitting cross-legged on the floor of Rafe's office. His laptop rested in front of her on a stack of green-and-white printouts. Rafe sat at a desk crowded with an impressive array of computer equipment, including three monitors displaying three different—and to Charlotte, equally indecipherable—screens of code. Cables crawled across the floor, connecting two scanners and three printers to one or the other of the two CPUs under Rafe's desk.

"I need the laptop when I travel. When I'm working here, I use one computer for downloads, the other for confidential work. It isn't hooked up to anything. That's basic security." Rafe flashed a grin at his friend. "There are too many people like Dix who are too curious for my own good."

"Nah," Dix retorted amiably. He lounged in an armchair in the corner. A board resting across the arms of the chair held his laptop. "Not like me. I'm the best."

Charlie was beginning to like Dix. When Rafe had told him that she would be working with them, he hadn't turned a hair, unlike Rafe's other friend. Before leaving, Luke Starwind had tried to talk Rafe out of letting her be part of the investigation. Maybe she couldn't blame him for being suspicious. He had given Rafe the name of a criminal defense attorney Charlie could use, and promised to contact him on her behalf. That didn't mean she had to like the man. Or trust him.

But Rafe trusted her. In spite of everything, he believed in her. She hugged that knowledge to herself like a child with a Christmas secret.

"So why haven't I read about you?" she asked Dix, smiling so he'd know she was teasing. "The hacker who was caught last month for getting into some top-secret files got great press."

He gave her a slow wink. "Little girl, I don't get caught. That's why I'm the best."

Rafe snorted. "No, that's because you've got better sense than to break into the Pentagon's system just to prove you can."

"Hey, man," Dix said. "Quit interrupting. I'm trying to flirt with your girlfriend."

"Work now, flirt later. Charlie, do you understand what you're looking for?"

"I think so. Files accessed after hours, frequently used access codes—the same sort of thing I was looking for on my own, but you've narrowed the possibilities."

"Okay. If you have any questions, ask Dix. He likes to show off."

She called up the first of the files she was supposed to check and began.

Rafe had run several diagnostics without turning up signs of tampering or any obvious problems. There were some flagged areas, though. She was slogging through user records. Rafe—well, she wasn't clear on exactly what he was doing. Something involving a special program he was writing, but he'd spoken of it in such technical terms he'd lost her. Fortunately, she didn't have to understand his job to do hers.

By two o'clock her back ached and her stomach was growling. The two men were obviously not plagued by the physical discomforts of lesser mortals. Aside from tossing each other an occasional question or comment in terms so technical they might as well have been Martian, they'd been silent the whole time.

Enough was enough. She yawned and stretched. "I don't know about you two, but I'm hungry."

"If you're offering to fix something," Dix said, "I'm accepting. I'm not picky. I'll eat anything I don't have to cook."

"I'll see if I can find some sandwich fixings. Rafe?"

No answer. He didn't even twitch.

Dix chuckled. "When he's really into a program, it's not easy to get his attention. Pain works. Though you do have to be fast on your feet if you use that approach."

"I'll try something a little less drastic first." She wadded up a piece of paper and lobbed it at Rafe.

It hit him on the neck. He swatted at it, as if a bug had bit him, and went right on working, his fingers flying over the keyboard. She laughed.

His fingers stopped. His head cocked to one side. "You don't do that often enough."

"What—throw things at you?"

"Laugh out loud." He swiveled. "Are you going to make sandwiches?"

"You did hear! Why didn't you answer?"

"It isn't that I don't hear things when I'm working. It all just goes somewhere else, where it won't interrupt my train of thought."

She smiled, amused. "Where does it go?"

"Damned if I know." He stood and stretched. "Tell you what. I'm ready for a break anyway. I'll make the sandwiches and you can put away the clothes Dix brought."

"Put them away where? You were going to clear out a couple of drawers for me, remember?"

"Move some of my stuff around. You'll do better at finding places for things than I would, anyway."

He asked Dix a question in Martian, and the two men were deeply involved in one of their jargon-laden conversations before Charlie left the room. She smiled as she went down the hall, wondering if either of them would remember to fix the sandwiches.

Two bulging garbage bags sat on the floor of Rafe's bedroom: packing, man-style. She wondered if Rafe even owned an iron. She couldn't afford to send everything to the cleaners just because it was wrinkled. Of course, a great deal of her wardrobe wouldn't fit anymore. She put a hand on her stomach, savoring the firm swelling. The baby stirred.

Something else was stirring inside her. It felt very much like hope.

Maybe, just maybe, she and Rafe could work out some kind of future together. He seemed to have forgiven her for her part in the Kellys' schemes without knowing how they'd forced her to cooperate. She thought he'd forgiven her for not telling him about the baby right away, too.

Maybe, she thought as she knelt beside one of the trash bags, some of his anxiety this morning *had* been for her. Maybe he really did care. Caring wasn't love, but it was a start.

He trusted her. He *believed* in her. Yes, the wiggly feeling inside felt very much like hope. Or happiness.

She worked the twist-tie loose and looked inside. Shoes. All her shoes were in there, dumped on top of jeans and sweaters. Her smile widened. There were advantages to a man who'd grown up with sisters, she thought, pulling out her favorite gray pumps.

Brad had grown up with a sister. It hadn't seemed to do him much good.

Her smile faded as she tensed against the familiar anxiety. Automatically she started pulling things out of the bag, making neat piles.

Charlotte had never been able to decide whether she'd done too much for Brad, or too little. Had she been too harsh, lectured him too often? Or had she just never said the right things? He was so different from her, so volatile. Her hands smoothed a sweater as a deep sadness welled up. The one thing she and her little brother had in common, other than the same set of parents, was a hunger for fine things. Perhaps if she'd been able to rise above her own material longings...

She shook her head and made her hands move briskly, unpacking, then changing into pants and a sweater of her own. Sometimes she was able to convince herself that Brad's descent into a mad, bad world wasn't her fault, that nothing she could have done would have helped him make different choices. Sometimes she couldn't. But she had been so very young when their parents died. Whatever mistakes she might have made, they were past altering now.

The biggest mistakes had been Brad's. She didn't fool herself about that. He'd been young when he made them, yes, but not too young to understand the consequences. Not too young to be tried as an adult.

He was paying for those mistakes now, but he shouldn't have to pay with his life.

Lieutenant Johnson had kept his word. In exchange for her testimony he'd arranged for Brad to be secretly moved to a different prison. Even she didn't know where he was. At least now she knew for sure that the lieutenant had kept as quiet about it as he'd warned her to be. *Tell no one he's been moved,* the SIU officer had said. *If the Kellys find him, he's dead.*

It hadn't been a difficult secret to keep…until now. She grimaced and opened the other trash bag. She'd moved to Chicago after Brad was sentenced. No one here knew her brother existed. It had seemed simpler that way, easier than answering a lot of questions about him…and, she admitted with a grimace, she'd been ashamed. Not of Brad, exactly. Of everything that she'd come from. The chance to reinvent herself had been irresistible. But now…

Now she thought she could tell Rafe about her brother. She frowned, her hands growing still. She'd refused to tell him earlier because she hadn't trusted him. Oh, not that she thought he would sell her brother out to the Kellys. But he had a nasty habit of doing what he thought was best and running right over anyone who objected. Look at the way he'd dragged her out of Hole-in-the-Wall last night.

And he'd told Luke Starwind everything. Charlie didn't exactly distrust Starwind, but she didn't exactly trust him, either. Not enough to put her brother's life in the man's hands.

Rafe apparently told Dix everything, too. And she wanted to trust Dix. She would have, if it had been just herself, just her own secrets she was keeping. If it weren't her brother's very life at stake, she would tell Rafe everything.

That was what he had said, too, wasn't it? When he'd told her she had to stay away while he and Dix tracked down what the Kellys had done to the computers. "If it was just me," he'd said. "If there weren't so many others involved..."

It had hurt.

Had she hurt him by refusing to trust him?

She chewed on her lip and thought about how good she'd felt when he changed his mind and decided to trust her. She thought about hope.

The wiggle-worm in her womb did a slow roll.

Making her mind up all at once, she pushed to her feet. She would make him promise, she thought, hurrying out of the room. Before she told him, she would have his promise not to repeat it to anyone—not Dix, not Starwind, not even his father. He might not like it. He might make an unholy pest of himself trying to change her mind. But he would keep his word if he gave it. She was sure of that.

The office was empty. She smiled as she went by. Apparently he and Dix had remembered the sandwiches. She went down the stairs carefully, since her socks didn't offer much traction on the iron risers.

They didn't make much noise, either. Certainly not enough for the two men to hear her coming, not when Rafe's voice was raised enough for her to hear him from the kitchen.

"Dammit, Dix, don't give me a hard time about this."

Her feet slowed but didn't stop. Maybe this wasn't a good time, if he and his friend were arguing. But if she didn't speak up now, she was afraid she'd talk herself out of it. It was too easy to keep things secret.

"...don't like it, that's all," Dix was saying. "She's a sweet little thing. I don't like lying to her."

Lying? Her feet kept moving, but she didn't notice. Her mind had gone numb.

"I didn't lie to her."

Dix snorted. "No, but you fancy-danced your way around the truth pretty good. She doesn't have a clue what's going on. She thinks she's really doing something, going through all those access records."

"That's where we found the clue. If she finds it, too…" Rafe's voice drifted off. "I need to know. If she spots the same thing we did—"

"Is that what this is about? You're testing her?"

Charlotte's feet kept right on moving. They carried her right up to the kitchen doorway. Then they stopped.

Rafe was leaning against the counter scowling at Dix, who stood a few feet away. He started to answer, then he saw her. Consternation and guilt spread across his face like a snail's slimy trail.

Hope lumped up in a cold, hard ball. And died.

"Charlie," he said, straightening. "Charlie, I can explain—"

She bolted.

Eight

He caught her, of course. Easily. She didn't even make it to the stairs before his hand landed on her shoulder, jerking her to a stop.

So she flung herself around and punched him. Right in the face.

That shocked her so much she froze. Her knuckles tingled. There was a red mark on his cheek, a mark she'd made.

He rubbed it. "Not bad, but you'd do better to aim for a less bony part of me next time. Noses are good. A nose won't hurt your hand the way a cheekbone will."

"Everything's a joke to you, isn't it?"

"Would you rather I hit you back? Look, I know at this point anything I say can and will be held against me, but I'd still like the chance to explain."

She folded her arms across her chest. "Go right ahead." Why not? He wasn't going to let her go until he did. So she waited, stone-faced, for him to explain why it had been necessary to trick her. To test her.

Test, not trust. Oh, what a fool she was. Over and over, she made a fool of herself with him.

Now that he had her attention, he didn't seem to know what to do with it. He looked away, rubbing his hand over his head as if he could rub some sense into it. "You looked so sad when I said you couldn't be around when Dix and I were working," he said at last. "I hated that."

"And you've made me so much happier by lying to me. Wonderful plan." She wanted to hit him again. Or cry. But she'd be damned before she let him see that, so she turned away.

Of course he stopped her. This time he grabbed her arm. "I was trying not to hurt you. Maybe I screwed up, but what do you expect? I don't know what I'm doing here! How can I do the right thing when I don't have a clue half the time what that is?" His voice was rising. "And you don't help. You want it all your way."

"Me?" Temper brought her around to face him once more. The hand she'd hit him with was beginning to throb. "I'm not the one who keeps physically dragging someone else around to get my way!"

"But you want the trust thing all your way, don't you? I'm supposed to trust you, and you're not supposed to have to tell me a damned thing!"

She'd been going to. She'd been ready to. Now... "I don't care if you trust me or not," she said, and at that moment she meant it. "I don't trust you, so it really doesn't matter how you feel about me, does it?"

Temper sparked in his eyes. His hand tightened on her arm. Then let go. He whirled and slammed his palm against the wall. "Dix!" he yelled. "Come tell this damned complicated woman what we're doing! Tell her everything! I'm going out!"

By the time Dix came out of the kitchen, the front door had slammed behind Rafe.

* * *

Rafe drove, paying no attention to where he went.

Charlie wasn't going to let him touch her any time soon. If he couldn't touch her, how could he persuade her to marry him? Hell, he'd be lucky if she didn't run again.

That would be all he needed, he fumed. To have to track her down again, praying with every hour that passed that he found her before the Kellys did. She wouldn't skip right away, though. She'd want to find out what was going on. Dix would be filling her in right about now.

Contrary to what he'd let Charlie believe, they already knew what the Kellys' tech had done. Broderton had planted a "back door" in the Connelly computers, one that allowed them untraceable access to the system. At least, it was supposed to have been untraceable. Rafe had found it and modified a program that logged user access to let him track the tech's activities. For the past four days he and Dix had been able to monitor everything the Kellys' tech did. The man—they assumed it was Broderton, the tech who had planted the worm in the Connelly system and had since vanished—was trying to get into a special partition in the mainframe where the most sensitive material was stored.

So far he hadn't been able to. The partition was heavily protected. Rafe had added some extra bells and whistles, so the data there should be safe—for a time. But what exactly the Kellys wanted with that data remained a mystery.

Which was why Rafe and Dix were working frantically on creating their own version of Broderton's worm. Rafe wanted to make it work in reverse—to follow the link the Kellys' tech opened right back to *their* computer. While Broderton tried to get into the secured partition, Rafe would be downloading every bit of data he could grab from the Kellys' system. Even crooks had to keep records. You couldn't manage any system without them. If Rafe was lucky, the tech might be using a computer that held those records—records of the crime family's activities that could be used to stop them once and for all.

Maybe. If everything went well. But Rafe's chances of turning the tables on the Kellys would vanish if the criminals had any idea what he was attempting. If he was wrong about Charlie…if the hold they had over her was stronger than her honor…

Someone had tried to kill his brother ten months ago. Someone was still trying to kill Charlie, and the Kellys were connected to both attempts. Rafe didn't know how, he didn't know why. He just knew they had to be stopped.

Maybe Charlie had told the truth when she said she wanted to fix what she'd allowed to happen. Maybe she could be trusted with his brother's life. He wanted to believe that.

And maybe she'd be so blind with hurt and anger because he'd tricked her that she would run again, and get herself—and their baby—killed.

Dammit. He couldn't keep her locked up. Tempting as that sounded, it wasn't a practical solution. He'd have to hope that whatever passed for reason in that convoluted brain of hers would accept that she was better off with him than on her own right now.

When you got right down to it, he didn't know why he was so angry with her. Charlie didn't trust him. So what? He'd known that. He'd been over the reasons for it in his mind plenty of times. She was a difficult, closed-up woman who didn't trust easily, and he'd already messed up once with her.

Now he'd screwed up again. Big-time. What was that saying about the road to hell and good intentions?

Rafe heaved a large sigh. Charlie needed to feel useful. He'd tried to give her that, but without gambling everything that the secrets she held on to so tightly wouldn't make her betray them all. He'd wanted to give her a chance, he told himself as he headed back up Lake Shore Drive. What was so wrong with that?

But giving someone a chance wasn't the same as trusting. Not when he gave with one hand and held back with the other. The look in her eyes when she'd come into the kitchen, silent as a ghost and almost as pale, that stayed with him. It kept him churned up after the anger faded.

He didn't think he'd ever been this confused in his life.

So maybe it shouldn't have surprised him when he realized where he'd wound up. But it did. He pulled up in his brother's parking space in the garage used by Connelly Corporation, shut off the engine, then just sat there, his mouth pulled into a thin, disgusted line.

Coming here wasn't a bad idea. He needed to fill his father in. He just wished it had been an actual decision, not some automatic-pilot trick he'd played on himself. Bad enough that he couldn't figure out what was going on with Charlie. Being clueless about his own actions was a real pain.

At least his blasted subconscious hadn't sent him to his parents' home. He did not want to run into his loving, all-too-perceptive mother. His phone call this morning would have primed the pump on her curiosity, and he did not want to be bombarded with questions. He wasn't in the mood for dealing with any females at the moment.

Rafe heaved another sigh, swung open the door and climbed out.

The woman who sat at Charlie's desk these days was named Martha "something or other." She was sharp as a tack, a cute little Puerto Rican spitfire. He hated seeing her where Charlie was supposed to be, so he took extra care to be nice. "Afternoon, Martha. I stopped by to see if you've changed your mind about running off with me."

She gave him a look over the top of her reading glasses. "My husband and I are free this weekend."

He shook his head. "No offense, but I doubt he'd be my type."

She laughed and waved at the door behind her. "Oh, go

on in. Your father doesn't have anyone with him right now.''

Rafe was frowning as he pushed open the door. The first time he'd seen Charlie at that desk she hadn't wanted to play with him at all. She'd looked so dubious about him, sitting there with her sunshine hair all smooth and pretty and her mouth all primmed up. So he'd asked her out. And he hadn't been teasing, though a second after the words came out, he'd pretended he was. It had been better that way. He didn't—

"Did you come to see me or to stare out my window?"

"Hi, Dad." Rafe turned toward the big desk and the big man who sat behind it. "I thought I'd better bring you up to date."

"You've made progress?" Grant leaned back in his chair.

Progress? Mostly of the backward sort. Rafe grimaced. His father wasn't asking about his matrimonial plans. "Some. This isn't a plain, garden-variety virus Dix and I are working on, you know. More of a worm with legs. The subroutines alone—"

"Never mind the technicalities. I won't understand them. You're sure the Kellys can't get into anything they shouldn't, in the meantime?"

"They can't get into the partition." Rafe moved restlessly around the office. Charlie had worked for his father for over two years. Grant Connelly probably knew her as well as anyone, and better than most. "They can wander around the rest of the records pretty freely if they decide to, but their tech hasn't shown an interest in anything but the partition since we've been monitoring him."

"How much longer will you need to finish that fancy program of yours?"

"Another week, maybe. Could be more."

Grant drummed his fingers on the arm of his chair. "For

the life of me I can't figure out what would be worth this much trouble to them. Starwind suggested it might be some kind of money-laundering scheme.''

Rafe shook his head. ''Luke's good at what he does, but he doesn't know computers. Nothing that's behind the partition would help them pass money secretly through your accounts.''

''And money laundering wouldn't explain the attempt on Daniel's life last January.''

''No.'' Rafe brooded over that. No one had been able to come up with any scenario, however far-fetched, that connected the Kellys' interest in the Connelly computers to what had seemed to be a purely political assassination attempt when Daniel inherited the Altarian throne.

But there was a dead man who'd found some kind of connection. Tom Reynolds.

Grant thrummed the arm of his chair again. ''One way or another we have to find out what they're after. What are your chances of pulling this off?''

''Good, as far as hitching a ride back to their computer goes. I can't guarantee we'll find anything useful. Broderton is no slouch. The worm he planted in your computers is a devilishly clever piece of work. If he's in a position to advise them—''

''Spare me,'' Grant said dryly, standing. ''You may admire your alter ego's technical prowess, but I can't summon appreciation for anyone connected to the Kellys. And something tells me you didn't come here to talk about Broderton, anyway.''

''Not entirely.'' He looked out the window, down at the floor, then finally met his father's gray eyes. ''Mom told you that I found Charlie, I guess. That she's staying with me.''

Grant nodded.

''I decided to let Charlie in on what's going on. Everything." When his father didn't respond, he shoved his hands in his pockets. "You must wonder why. Considering she's the reason the Kellys were able to plant the worm in the first place."

"I suppose you have a reason."

"Probably." Rafe sighed. "I wish I knew what the hell it was. Listen," he said, beginning to pace. "You didn't press charges against her. What do you think—was she forced to do it? She won't tell me anything. Not one damned thing. Do I know where she went to school? What her childhood was like? No and no. How about what the Kellys threatened her with? No. What she thinks she's going to do if she doesn't marry me? Hell, no."

He stopped and glared at his father. "She wouldn't tell me the sky was blue without a subpoena. Why are women so blasted unreasonable?"

"It's the estrogen. Makes their emotions jumpy, so they think that's normal. And if you tell your mother I said that, I'll disown you." Grant went to the small wet bar in the corner and poured himself and his son a shot of scotch, neat. "I take it things aren't going smoothly with Charlotte."

Rafe gave a short laugh. "You could say that." He accepted the drink, eyed it briefly, then tossed it down.

"Good God. That's no way to treat seventeen-year-old whiskey."

The burn robbed him of breath for a moment. Whether the alcohol cleared his mind or not, it worked wonders for his sinuses. "I'm in an excessive mood."

"So I see. Do you want to tell me why you really came here?"

"Not especially." He studied the empty shot glass, turning it around and around. When he'd told his parents he was going to marry Charlie, his mother had looked worried and asked him if that was what he truly wanted. His father had simply nodded as if he'd been expecting it.

Probably he had. Grant Connelly knew his sons pretty well.

Rafe moved restlessly to the window. From up here the city looked busy but orderly. Down on the streets, noise and confusion took over. Rafe liked being able to have it both ways—the lively, in-your-face bustle of the streets, and the chance to pull back into his own space when the crowds and clamor got to him.

He felt a lot the same about his family. He loved them, couldn't imagine life without them, but they were a close, pushy bunch. He needed to be able to get away from them as much as he sometimes needed them around. That's why he didn't work for Connelly Corporation.

Charlie didn't have a family. Maybe that was why she was always pulling back, opting for distance and order. She didn't know how to handle the up-close-and-personal.

He frowned at the distant, orderly scene below. "When you first found out what Charlie had done, you were mad as blue blazes. But you didn't want her charged as an accessory. In fact, you put pressure on the police so they wouldn't charge her."

"I didn't want her to go to jail. I've always liked Charlotte. I consider her a woman of high principles. But sometimes when principles and need clash, need wins. I'd like to know what need the Kellys used against her."

So would he. If he could just be sure, absolutely sure, it hadn't been money... "I thought she might have told you."

"I haven't spoken with her since the police brought her in for questioning after Reynolds was killed."

Rafe considered pouring another shot, then decided against it. He hadn't come here to drink. Or to talk about Broderton and the Kellys, as his father had pointed out. "I guess I was wondering how you feel about me marrying her."

"She's carrying your baby. It's the right thing to do." Grant sipped his scotch. "More importantly, how do you feel about it?"

"She's making me crazy. I don't know what to do about it. She turned me down, you know."

His father hesitated. "I'm sorry to hear that. Will she agree to a joint custody arrangement?"

Rafe waved that aside. "She's going to marry me. I haven't worked out how to persuade her, but I will."

"I'm not sure what you want me to tell you, then. Are you looking for advice on how to persuade her?"

Rafe wasn't sure what he was looking for, either. Nothing he could imagine putting into words. *How did you and Mom work things out after she found out about Seth? How did you put the pieces back together after you'd made a royal mess of them?* But they had never talked about that sort of thing. His parents had separated, his father had had an affair and then they'd gotten back together, and Rafe didn't have the foggiest idea how it had all gone wrong or been put right again. Or how to bring up a subject that was off-limits.

He tried asking obliquely. "How do you get a woman to trust you?"

"By being someone she can trust."

Rafe flicked his father a hard look. There had been a time when Grant hadn't been someone his wife could trust, but somehow he'd gotten past that. Somehow he and Rafe's mother had gone from fractured to strong and solid, and Rafe would have appreciated a more substantial hint on how to work that bit of magic.

"Never mind," he said abruptly. "I'll work it out." He glanced at the door, hesitated, then asked one more question. "Has Charlie ever mentioned someone named Brad Fowler to you?"

"Fowler." Grant gave the name a few moments' thought. "No, I don't believe so. But she never said much about her personal life. She's a very private person."

No kidding. Rafe turned to go. "Thanks for the drink."

"Rafe."

He paused at the door, looking over his shoulder. "Yeah?"

"In many ways you take after your mother. As your sister Maggie would say, you're a 'people person.' You enjoy getting your way, but you lack my, ah, tendency to try to control others. You're like me in one way, though. Once you've made up your mind you want something, you go after it with everything you have. It's not a bad trait, but I can tell you from experience it can make you blind sometimes."

Rafe frowned, puzzled and annoyed. "If you have a point, I wish you'd make it."

"You're determined to marry Charlotte."

"You agreed it's the right thing to do."

Grant smiled faintly. "Yes, but I don't think that's why you're hell-bent on getting married."

"I'm not hell-bent on getting married. I don't want to be married. I do want my child, and I want him or her to have two parents who live together."

"And Charlotte? Do you want her, too?"

"She didn't get pregnant all by herself," Rafe growled. "Of course I want her. That doesn't mean I'm crazy about marriage. It's the right thing to do, that's all."

"Hmm. Well, like I said, there's nothing wrong with going after what you want. But you need to decide if you're using the woman to get the baby, or using the baby to get the woman. Neither one is likely to work out well."

After his son had left, Grant stood by the window for several minutes, sipping his scotch and thinking.

At sixty-five, Grant Connelly looked like what he was— a man who possessed money and power, and was comfortable with both. He favored suits tailored for him, Italian shoes and frequent manicures, all of which put an attractive gloss on the predator beneath. A man didn't climb to the top of a competitive, often ruthless heap and stay there for nearly forty years without his own share of ruthlessness— and that tendency he'd mentioned to his son. Emma had told him more than once that his habit of trying to control those around him arose from sheer, bloody arrogance, the unconscious assumption that he was always right.

But a good businessman knows when to call in the experts. After a few minutes of frowning contemplation he moved back to his desk, picked up the phone and called his wife.

Nine

Rafe left his father's office in a worse state of confusion than he'd been in when he'd arrived. Damn, but he hated it when his dad turned all wise and cryptic. Why couldn't he just come out and say what he meant?

Using the baby to get the woman. Using the woman to get the baby. What was that supposed to mean? Rafe didn't see any reason he couldn't have them both. That was the whole idea.

Right now, though, he was about as far from becoming a reluctantly married man as he'd ever been. He'd be lucky if Charlie was speaking to him when he got home. If she did speak, he thought gloomily, she'd be using that polite voice of hers. The one that meant she was up in her tower, safely distant from all the noise and confusion.

If he had to live with all this confusion, she would just have to get down in the messy middle of things, too. It was only fair.

Charlie did like things tidy, though. By now she would

have found some nice, neat label to hang on him, something along the lines of Tricky—Don't Trust. His father thought he needed to prove he could be trusted, but Rafe didn't have time for that. Charlie was a stubborn woman. She'd hang on to that label she'd stuck on him halfway to forever if he let her.

The thing to do, he decided, was to be every bit as tricky as she thought he was—and then some.

"You sure I can't get you something before I go?" Dix asked. He stood at the door to the office with his laptop in one hand and a ferocious frown on his face. "Some juice, maybe?"

"Quite sure, thank you." Charlotte kept her head bent over the printout Dix had given her earlier. It listed the name and a brief précis of all the files stored within the partition the Kellys' tech was trying to get into. Somewhere in these files was the answer. It had to be.

"You should eat something."

"I will," she assured him. "I'm not hungry yet, but I'll fix something later." *Leave. Please leave now.*

"Okay. See you tomorrow." Still he hesitated.

She glanced up finally and met his eyes. "I *will* be here tomorrow. I promised I wouldn't leave, and I'm not a fool. I came here because I had nowhere else to go, and that's still true."

His frown didn't go away, but he nodded and, at last, he left. She listened to his steps on the stairs and took a deep breath—the first unobserved breath she'd had since Rafe slammed out of the apartment.

Dix looked tough. He talked tough. But he was a real marshmallow, she'd discovered. He'd been driving her crazy all afternoon, sneaking worried looks at her, as if he thought she was going to fall apart. Good grief. She was perfectly fine. Just because she and Rafe had had an argument...that was no big deal. They'd argued before. Perhaps she had been rather emotional, but she'd had plenty of time to calm down. Rafe had been gone for hours. She...

Was shaking. With a sense of betrayal Charlotte looked at the trembling hand holding a pencil. She couldn't write. She could barely hold the pencil.

Her eyes closed. There was a horrid, jittery feeling inside her, as if she'd drunk three pots of coffee in a row. Or was sitting in the dentist's chair with her mouth wedged open, watching helplessly as the drill came closer and closer. The dreadful feeling had been coming over her in waves all afternoon. It would retreat for a while and she'd think she'd finally pulled herself together—then, just as she was managing to concentrate, it would start shaking its way out again.

She set down the pencil with a sigh. It was very upsetting. Work had always been her sanctuary. Before moving to Chicago she'd handled the bookkeeping for a few small businesses. She didn't know how she would have made it through Brad's arrest and trial if she hadn't had all those soothing columns of figures to submerge herself in every night.

Why wasn't work helping now?

Pregnancy hormones, she thought, pushing to her feet and moving to Rafe's desk. She'd read that they caused a lot of emotional swings. She just had to ride this mood out. Sooner or later she'd settle down again. In the meantime, she could darned well get some work done. Whether it soothed her wasn't as important as contributing to the effort to catch the Kellys.

She sat in Rafe's chair and bent to slide a CD into its drive.

Why had he done it? Why had Rafe told Dix to tell her what he and Dix were really working on?

Her hand paused in midair. Her mouth turned down. This wasn't the first time that thought had intruded on her concentration. Deliberately she completed the motion.

The CD contained software to link to the Connelly computers. She waited through the dialing beeps, tapping her fingers impatiently.

She just couldn't make sense of Rafe's abrupt turn-around. He'd carefully kept the truth from her—and now that she wasn't blinded by emotion, she could understand why. She'd wanted him to trust her on some emotional level, but that would be irresponsible. Logic as well as feeling confirmed that Rafe couldn't be in league with the Kellys. If they had been able to use him, they wouldn't have needed their elaborate machinations to gain access to the Connelly computers. He could have handed them whatever they wanted, and no one would ever have been the wiser.

The same couldn't be said of her. Rafe had every reason to doubt and very little to trust.

Test, not trust.

Charlie's fingers stilled as anger spiked through her again. He should have left it alone. After asking her to stay downstairs when he and Dix were working, he should have let the subject drop. He shouldn't have pretended to trust. He…

Had changed his mind.

She bit her lip. Rafe had been so furious that he'd attacked an unsuspecting wall—and then he'd yelled at Dix to tell her everything. Why? It wasn't as if he were the sort to cave in under opposition. Oh, no. Normally you couldn't change that man's mind with a two-by-four. He was hard-headed, confident, so sure he was right….

But maybe he wasn't sure with her.

Charlie's heartbeat picked up. The shaky feeling was back, stronger than ever. Damn him, he was messing with her mind and she wanted him *out*. She wanted to have her thoughts to herself again. Why couldn't he leave her alone, even when she was alone? She—wasn't alone. At the sound of voices downstairs, her heart jumped. One of them was Rafe. She knew his voice, even if she couldn't make out the words from up here. Her heartbeat settled back to normal.

But who was with him? She heard a male voice, and a female one, too. A scraping noise, as if something was being moved. Laughter, and—what was that? *Drums?*

More voices. A muffled thud.

What in the world was the dratted man up to? Surely he wasn't giving a party! Well, whatever he was doing, she was not going to gratify him by going downstairs to find out. She didn't want to see him, speak to him or think about him. She'd stay up here and by damn, she would get some work done.

She called up a directory. Downstairs someone was tuning up an instrument. With an extreme effort of will Charlie managed to focus on the screen, even to make a little progress. She was almost able to tune out the strange sounds coming from downstairs—the buzzer sounding, more scraping sounds as if furniture was being moved, people talking...

"Charlie!" Rafe called. "Stay up there a few minutes longer, okay? Don't come down yet."

She was in the hall when the tiki music started playing. Tiki music?

Rafe stood at the foot of the stairs. He was wearing the same dark blue turtleneck and torn jeans he'd had on earlier, but he'd added something. Flowers. Two gaudy tropical leis hung around his neck.

He grinned. "I knew telling you to stay put would bring you running."

Her mouth flattened. She almost turned around and went back up the stairs. Too predictable, she told herself.

Besides, by then she'd seen too much to turn back.

Most of the lights had been turned off. The music came from a trio of musicians wearing sarongs and flowers. Or maybe the men's costumes weren't called sarongs. Whatever the name for the cloth around their hips, it was short and flowered and left a lot of coppery skin bare. One of the men was playing drums; another played some sort of flute, while the woman strummed a stringed instrument. Another man—this one older and fully clothed in a white dinner jacket and dark slacks—was setting the table. Not the dining table. The coffee table. Which had been moved in front of the fireplace...and the palm tree.

A real, live palm tree leaned over the coffee table. Pots of exotic flowers circled it. The man in the white dinner jacket was lighting candles, and a fire burned in the fireplace. The sweet scent of flowers mingled with spicy, unfamiliar aromas from the food the waiter had set out.

She stood on the last step and stared. "You *are* having a party."

"You could call it that." He held out his hand. "Or you could call it an apology."

Her heart was beating too hard. She could feel it pounding in her throat, keeping time with the drums. She swallowed and ignored his outstretched hand. "I don't understand."

"You know what I'm apologizing for, so it must be the manner of the apology you don't understand." The smile hung on his lips as he dropped his hand back to his side, but his eyes were dark. Serious. "I've been too narrowly focused, you see. I kept thinking you're too secretive, that you won't tell me anything. But I've learned some things about you in the past two years."

The smile eased into his eyes. "For example, I know you enjoy Italian food, Mexican food and the opera. You had a dog named Beau when you were thirteen—you told me that when I mentioned the dog I had when I was a kid. I know you like pretty clothes and a clean desk, and you're nuts about organizing things. You've got the sexiest mouth I've ever seen, and you've never been to Hawaii."

The sexiest mouth? Her tongue came out to touch her lips. She realized what she was doing and cleared her throat. "Ah, Hawaii. I mentioned that last year. That's why you sent me that silly doll when you went there on a business trip.''

He nodded and lifted one of the leis over his head. "I nearly sent you a postcard—you know, the sort that say, 'Thinking of you, wish you were here.' Because I was, and I did. But I didn't want to be thinking about you. It bugged me. So I sent you the doll instead.''

He moved even closer, so that only inches separated them. His voice dropped. "I also know you're honest to a fault. You don't lie, you don't cheat or steal or bend the rules. If you say that whatever hold the Kellys had on you isn't an issue anymore, then it isn't. I wish you'd trust me enough to tell me about it, though.''

He paused, giving her a chance to speak, to tell him. She firmed her lips against the urge to do so. All along she'd been too easy for him. She'd fallen into bed with him. She'd let him drag her back to his apartment. And now—now, she thought with a flutter of panic, she was close to forgiving him for everything. For anything, so long as he kept looking at her that way.

No. She wasn't so weak, so foolishly female. A few pretty words proved nothing. He'd known her for two years, just as he said. And for two years he'd found her eminently resistible. Rafe wanted his child, he wanted to have things his way, and he didn't mind seducing her to get it. Her jaw tightened, locking the words inside.

"No?" he said softly. "Well, I can't blame you. I'm sorry I didn't trust you earlier.'' He settled the lei over her head, and the heady scent of jasmine drifted up to tease her. "I didn't take you to Hawaii with me last year, Charlie. My mistake. Let me bring Hawaii to you tonight.''

She liked the hula dancer. Rafe smiled at her astonishment, and at the suspicious look she cast him. She was sure she had his number. She thought she knew how the evening would end—with him trying to get her into bed.

And Lord knew that was how he wished it could end.

She was like wine, Charlie was, flowing sweetly through
his veins and making him ache. But for tonight, at least,
neither of them would get what they wanted. He wouldn't
seduce her because that was what she was expecting. And
she wouldn't keep him tucked neatly in whatever mental
pigeonhole she'd assigned him.

The way past Charlie's walls was to keep her off-
balance.

In the meantime, he was enjoying her reactions. By the
time the hula dancer finished and the waiter removed the
salad plates and began serving the main course, Charlie was
in trouble. She wasn't being polite at all.

She fussed at him, telling him he was an idiot and this
was absurdly extravagant. Her eyes were glowing. He
agreed and urged her to try the *moloka'i*, the famous sweet
rolls from the islands. She shook her head, took a greedy
bite, swallowed and said she didn't even want to think
about how much all this had cost. And her eyes were soft,
beginning to dream.

She made a face when she tried the poi, but the lomi-
lomi salmon and guava chicken went over big. The real hit
of the evening, though, arrived as they were finishing des-
sert. Just when he'd decided the theatrical agent hadn't
been able to come through, the last act showed up.

Charlie *loved* the sword dancers.

She watched, mouth open, as the two muscular young
men in grass loincloths and fancy headdresses pranced and
gyrated and tossed swords back and forth in Rafe's darkened living room. And Rafe watched her.

"Equal opportunity ogling," he said, leaning close to be
heard over the pounding drums. "I watched a pretty woman
wiggle her hips while we ate our salads, so it's only fair
you get to look at a couple of naked men."

She ducked her head and glanced at him sideways.
"Nearly naked," she corrected, a smile nipping at the corners of her mouth, as if she knew a secret that pleased her.

Maybe she'd noticed that he'd been looking at her, not the hula dancer.

Or maybe that sideways glance was the come-hither his body wanted it to be. Down, boy, he told himself. No point in raising hopes—and other things—that weren't going to be fulfilled tonight.

Naturally, his body paid no attention to reason. He leaned back and shifted, trying to ease the increasing pressure his jeans were putting on a sensitive part of his anatomy.

After the drums and the dancers had crashed into a grand finale, he applauded, though he had no idea if the performance had been any good. He'd been too busy watching Charlie. Judging by the way she was making her palms sting, though, she thought they'd been great. He smiled. "Want to honeymoon on Oahu?"

Her eyebrows twitched and her mouth tried to get prim again. "Rafe—"

"We'll talk in a minute," he promised, rising. "I've got to reward these fellows for a great show."

He ushered out the performers and the waiter, suitably enriched for their efforts, and hit the last light switch on his way back to Charlie. The room faded into nearly complete darkness. Candles still flickered on the table, but the fire had died down to a few small flames licking along the remains of the logs. Most of the light came from the big, undraped window where Charlie now stood—city lights filtered by the fronds of his new palm tree.

Charlie was looking out the window with her arms hugged across her chest. Battle stations, he thought, smiling. She was primed and ready to repel his advances.

"I hope you've got a green thumb," he said when he reached her.

"What?" Her hair was rebelling against that tight ponytail she'd pulled it into. Lots of wiggly bits had already escaped. Absently she tucked one of the escapees behind her ear. "A green thumb? Why?"

He liked the way all those loose curls tickled her face

and frisked around on her neck. He wanted to play with them. He shoved his hands into his pockets instead. "Because I'll probably kill it," he said, nodding at the palm. "I don't have a good track record with plants."

"Oh. Well, I don't know much about palm trees, but I can find out. There are probably resources on the Net about that sort of thing. Gardening books, too. There are bound to be books about palm trees. Or tropical plants. At bookstores, I mean, not the Internet. Or libraries. I—" She grimaced. "I'm babbling."

"Yeah. It's cute." Unfortunately, shoving his hands in his pockets had put more strain on his jeans right where he didn't need it. He pulled his hands out again. One of them immediately took advantage of that freedom to touch a playful wisp near her cheek. "I like your hair this way."

She frowned, but it wasn't very successful. Her eyes were too luminous in the glow from the fire and the city for effective frowning. "Messy, you mean?"

"I like you messy." His thumb got the idea to stroke her cheek. Such soft skin she had. "I like you tidy, too, but that may be because it makes me fantasize about messing you up. Did you know that when you're working, you get this little vee of concentration right here?" He smoothed the spot between her brows with one finger. "It makes me nuts."

Her laugh was unsteady. She took a step back. "You *are* nuts."

Her lower lip couldn't decide if it wanted to turn up or down. Her breath seemed to be in a hurry, which had a delightful effect on her breasts. His gaze lingered there, then returned to her face.

She was biting that undecided lower lip, but her eyes were steady and wide open when they met his. And it hit him suddenly. He could have her. Tonight. *Now.* If he put out his hand, touched her, pushed just a little, she would topple. She wanted to topple. Whether Charlie knew it or not, she was ready to be seduced into doing what they both wanted.

His breath stuck in his chest. His hands grew warm. His pulse took over his body, a hard throbbing that rushed from groin to stomach to neck. All along he'd told himself he would have her in his bed soon—but this wasn't soon. This was *now*. The sudden certainty of her acceptance was a lure he wasn't sure he could resist.

So why he said what he did, he had no idea. "Maybe you should go upstairs."

She blinked. "Excuse me?"

"I'm having a hard time remembering that I wasn't going to seduce you. That's not supposed to be part of the program, but I'm very close to changing my mind." Or whatever passed for his mind at the moment.

"I see." Her eyelids dipped. The tip of her tongue touched her upper lip, then retreated back inside her mouth. "Apparently we were on the same wavelength for once. You weren't going to seduce me, and I wasn't going to let you. The thing is…" She put her hand squarely on the center of his chest. "I did change my mind."

"Ah…"

"Your heart is beating hard. You haven't been running, and I know you aren't afraid." She looked up at him. "So you must want me."

But he *was* afraid. The realization jolted him—what could he possibly be afraid of? He pressed his hand over hers, trapping it against the rapid thud of his heart. "Yeah. I want you."

"You don't sound happy about it."

He wasn't. He didn't like tasting the sour backwash of fear when there was nothing to be afraid of. But he was more aroused than angry. "Let's see if we can make me happy, then."

Slowly, giving her time to change her mind—knowing she wouldn't, and so damned turned on by the knowledge he could have pushed inside her that very second—he pulled her to him.

Ten

She had time.

Rafe moved his hands deliberately along the curve of her back, drawing her to him, giving her an eternity of seconds to tell him no, that he'd misunderstood or she'd changed her mind and she wasn't going to do this. Time enough to feel each of his fingers through the scant protection of her sweater, to thrill to the heat and pressure along her breasts and belly as their bodies touched. Plenty of time to wonder why he was angry—and just when she'd lost her mind.

She wasn't going to stop him. She wanted this, wanted him. Her heart was pounding as if it was trying to break free of the safe cage of her ribs and dance naked in the air.

Then his mouth was on hers. Hot, still angry—and oh, so welcome. Time shifted, slanted, becoming a dizzy rush of seconds slipping summer-warm through her blood as she tasted him again.

His mouth was as deliberate as his hands had been, his lips and tongue laying claim to hers insistently, as if she might still deny him. Her arms went around him as she sought the places she'd tried so hard not to remember in all the long nights since he'd left her. The hard slope of his shoulder. The dip of his spine, outlined by muscle. The way those muscles moved beneath her hands as his arms went tight around her, and his mouth turned greedy.

When their lips at last parted, they were both breathless. She tucked her head in the spot that seemed made for it, the warm hollow between his neck and his shoulder, and breathed him in. Her pulse sang. Between her legs, she throbbed.

He wrapped one hand in her hair and rested his head against hers. "I don't think I'm going to make it upstairs."

"No," she agreed, and then, because she had to, she added, "There's just one thing..."

His fingers tightened in her hair. "You're not changing your mind again."

"No. At least...I don't want to." She wasn't sure she could. She might be able to resist the sweet insistence of her body. She might find the strength to refuse the promised completion of his body. But his scent... How could she have come to need the simple smell of him in only one night? "But I have to be sure we understand each other. That it's...like last time. No expectations."

His head jerked up. "What the hell does that mean?"

She raised her head so she could meet his eyes. He was staring down at her, haughty as a king confronted by lèse-majesté. For some reason his arrogance didn't bother her this time. Instead, she wanted to soothe the tight muscles around his eyes. "The same thing it meant when you said it five months ago."

"Everything's changed since then." His hand left her hair, dropping to cup the swell of her stomach. "You're expecting my child. That gives me the right to expect some things from you. You damned well ought to expect certain things from me, too."

Temper nipped. "Like marriage, you mean." She pulled

back, but his arms tightened, holding her in place. "As far as you're concerned, our relationship is defined by the baby I'm carrying."

"I think you think you just said something significant, but damned if I know what you're getting at. Of course the baby changed things."

"What if it wasn't yours?"

His eyebrows snapped down. "If you're trying to tell me I'm not the father—"

"No." Aching in too many ways, she closed her eyes. He had no idea what she was trying to say. What she wanted him to say. "I'm not trying to tell you that."

"Good. Because I wouldn't believe you. Dammit, Charlie." The words were rough, but his voice softened. The arms around her gentled until he was holding her again, not pinning her in place. He sighed. "Why do you have to be so complicated?" His hand came up to urge her head back onto his shoulder.

She let him have his way, since it put her right where she wanted to be. "I suppose you're not?"

"I'm a simple man," he assured her, stroking her hair.

She almost laughed. Simple? Rafe was the most complex, confusing man she'd ever known. But the slow stroke of his hand stirred her, and the deep ache of her body gripped her too tightly for laughter.

He nuzzled the hair away from her ear and kissed the top of her jaw. "I'm just a man, after all, and we're pretty basic creatures, verging on simpleminded at times. Like right now. I'm having a hard time thinking of anything except ravishing you. Thoroughly. On the couch, or upstairs in my bed. Or on the stairs on the way to my bed. Or all three."

"On the stairs?" A laugh did make its way out, brief and shaky. She lifted her head to smile into his eyes. "I don't think so. That sounds terribly uncomfortable."

"Okay." He dropped a quick kiss on the corner of her mouth, then another on her cheek. "We'll skip the ravish-

ing on the stairs. Two out of three works for me. For now.''
He drew his hands down along her arms to capture her
hands. ''Have we talked enough to satisfy your female need
for words? Can we go on to the kind of communication a
crude male like me understands?''

His words were casual. His smile was lightly mocking,
though whether it mocked her or himself she didn't know.
But his eyes held heat and hunger and a need she had no
defense against.

The important part of what he was telling her was word-
less, so she answered the same way. She pressed herself
against him, going up on tiptoe so she could reach for his
mouth with hers.

Rafe met her more than halfway.

He groaned. His arms were tight around her, his mouth
demanding. And she gave herself up to the moment—and
him.

When his mouth left hers to trace her jaw, seeking the
pulse in her throat, she shivered and arched her neck. His
tongue traced that arc while his hands chased the shivers
his mouth created. Time broke into soap bubble moments,
floating and fragile, that burst, one after another, showering
her with sensation.

His mouth on hers, his tongue dancing, thrusting. Her
hands hunting for skin beneath the soft knit of his shirt.
His hand finding her breast beneath the sweatshirt, caress-
ing, teasing. The need building, the empty place waiting
for him, calling for him.

''Too many clothes,'' she gasped in a moment when her
mouth was, briefly, free.

''And too vertical,'' he agreed. Her feet left the ground
as he swung her up in his arms. She might have told him
she was too heavy if he'd given her a chance. But his mouth
stopped any protests before she could make them.

Then he was lowering her to the couch, coming down
on top of her, nestled between her legs. He kissed her wild,
kissed her boneless, then tore his mouth away. ''Is there

anything I should know?'' He smoothed her sweatshirt up over the swell of her belly. ''I don't want to hurt you. I don't want to do anything wrong.''

She smiled. ''My breasts are a little tender. Other than that, you can't hurt me. When I'm farther along…'' But that was in the future, and only dreamers concerned themselves with the future. All she and Rafe were offering each other was now. So she ran her hand down his side, around to his front—and up the full, hard length of him.

The cords in his neck went taut as his head went back. What he muttered might have been a curse or a prayer. His hips moved, pressing him firmly into her palm. ''I'm not going to make it if you do that.''

She squeezed gently.

''That's it. You're in trouble now.'' He pulled her hand away, pushed her sweatshirt up and tugged it over her head. He pushed her bra up without bothering to unfasten it— and bent his head.

His mouth was warm and sweet. First he licked, then gently closed his lips around her nipple. His slow sucking drew a tight band from breast to groin, making her moan. ''You're right,'' she gasped. ''Big trouble.'' She threaded her hands through his hair, but the ache was building too fast. Sweet as his mouth was, it wasn't enough.

His hands were busy, though, unfastening this and that, colliding with hers when she tried to help. Between them they managed to get her bra and his shirt off in spite of stopping to kiss whatever portion of each other's bodies they could reach, then her pants and panties.

He cupped her. She jolted and nearly tumbled him off. He slid a finger in. ''I've thought of doing this so often.'' Two fingers, and he was looking at her. ''The first time I saw you, looking so pretty and tidy at your desk, this is what I was thinking of doing.'' In and out. ''Could you tell? Is that why you looked so disapproving?'' His thumb lightly circled her clitoris and she bit her lip to keep back a cry. ''Did you ever think about me touching you like this when you were sitting there with your blouse buttoned up to your neck?'' Out and in.

''No,'' she said, and grabbed his arm, holding on tight. ''Maybe. I don't know. Dammit, Rafe...''

''Maybe?'' Sweat darkened his hairline and his chest heaved, but he remained intent on his intimate teasing. ''I think you do know. I think you thought about me sometimes, nasty thoughts about things like this....'' And he put three fingers in this time. ''And this.''

Her hips bucked. She gasped, grabbed his zipper and yanked it down. ''Stop playing! I want you in me.''

He looked up at her face and grinned, though it was strained. ''Now there's an idea.''

He tugged his jeans and briefs off. Then he was on top of her, easing her legs wider, easing himself inside. And she was full at last, full of Rafe, holding him inside. She made a sound, a sob.

''Charlie,'' he said, leaning forward to rest his forehead on hers, taking some of his weight on his arms. His skin was hot and slightly damp. ''You feel so good, Charlie. So good.''

She reached up with both hands, threading her fingers through his hair, cherishing the line of his jaw. She was all but panting in her need for the rest of the act, yet couldn't bear to move past this moment yet, when he was fully hers.

Suddenly afraid—and not wanting to know what she feared—she lifted her hips. He groaned and began to move, one slow thrust at a time.

Slow didn't work for either of them for long. The power built, cycling back and forth between them—his strength, her suppleness, her hands clutching, one of them moaning. Climax hit like a fist, a gut-punch of pleasure. She cried out. He slammed into her one more time and threw his head back, every muscle of his body clenched as he spilled his seed inside her.

Slowly he sank down, carefully keeping his weight off her stomach. He ended up with one of his legs between hers, his body angled across her hips, the rest of him on the couch. Her eyes closed. Little tingles chased themselves up her legs. Aftershocks shivered through her most intimate muscles.

His head was next to hers. She felt his breath stir her hair when he spoke softly. "Charlie."

That was all he said, just her name. But the way he said it made her smile, eyes still closed, drifting in a moment she wished would never end. He drifted with her, holding her close as her heartbeat gradually settled back to normal.

Eventually he spoke again. "I hate to mention this, but I'm about to fall off the couch."

Amusement made her open her eyes and slant him a sleepy glance. "I guess you want me to move over. Let me see if anything's working yet." She lay utterly still for a few seconds. "Nope. Apparently not."

"Lazy wench." He shifted and she accommodated him, and she ended up mostly on top of him with their legs tangled together. His fingers sifted through her hair. There was a dreamy contentment in being quiet and close this way, the demands of their bodies temporarily subdued. She felt the baby move, and smiled.

"Charlie."

There was an odd note in his voice. She opened her eyes. "Yes?"

"Your stomach is moving."

"Properly speaking, it isn't my stomach that's moving."

"Sweet God," he said, and put his hand on her belly.

His voice, even more than his words, made her look at him. She'd never seen that expression before—not on Rafe's face.

"Will it do that again?" he asked. "Can you get it to move again?"

"No. I don't…" Something was clutching at her, a hard squeezing as if she were about to cry. Which made no sense. She swallowed. "I can't make the baby move when I want. Or stop moving, for that matter. That's a whole separate little person in there, and he or she does what she or he wants to. But the baby will probably move again if you wait awhile.''

He waited, his fingers outstretched, as motionless as if he were trying to coax some small, timid creature out of hiding. When the baby rewarded his patience by squirming, a grin spread over his face. ''How about that.''

His delight made her unsteady, as if the shaky feeling that had plagued her all afternoon was coming back. Charlie swallowed and made herself breathe evenly. There was nothing wrong. There was no reason to feel panic nibbling at the edges.

''How does it feel to you when the baby moves?'' he asked.

''Pretty wonderful.''

''I guess it's not very big yet.'' He glanced at her face, frowning. ''But it's going to get bigger. It's got to hurt. When the baby comes out, I mean.''

''Yes, it will.'' *I'm fine. This mood will pass. It's just another ride on the hormone roller coaster.* ''I'm tough, though. I may scream a lot or curse, but I'll be fine.''

''I don't like it. There ought to be a better way, something that doesn't hurt. With all the advances in medical technology these days—''

She laughed, and it eased the tightness in her chest. ''Oh, Rafe. They tried the 'no pain' approach in the fifties, drugging women into unconsciousness. Mother Nature's way really works best for both mother and child.''

His mouth twisted ruefully. ''Am I getting carried away? All of a sudden everything is so real to me. I mean, I knew the baby was real. But before, we hadn't been introduced, me and the little squirmer here.'' His hand moved over her belly as if he could caress the life inside. ''Now we have.''

Her eyes stung. She hadn't planned to become pregnant, nor had she carefully selected her baby's father. Yet for all her lack of planning, she'd chosen well. Rafe was a good man. He would be a good father.

"Hey." He touched her cheek. "What's wrong? You're getting damp."

She blinked the moisture away. "Hormones. They make me a little crazy sometimes."

The lift of his eyebrow said he didn't buy that, but he let it pass. "Why don't you know if it's a girl or a boy? I thought they could tell these days."

"Usually they figure it out when they do an ultrasound, but I haven't had one yet. My doctor was going to do one when I was twenty-four weeks along, but...well, I missed that appointment."

"Because you went into hiding." His voice flattened. "You need to see another doctor right away. And I don't want to hear any nonsense about how women have been having babies for centuries without a doctor. They didn't all live through it."

"Don't worry. I'm all in favor of modern medicine." She bit her lip and looked down at his hand, still spread possessively over her stomach. "But it isn't that simple. I don't dare send for my medical records. I don't know if they could find me that way. I don't know how they found me the last time."

Rafe's mouth tightened. "I'll take care of it."

"I'm sure you mean well, but what do you know about obstetricians and how—"

"I'll find out. But this is the wrong time for this discussion, isn't it?" All at once he stood and slid one arm under her knees and the other behind her back.

She was so startled she squeaked as she rose in the air. That annoyed her, so she frowned at him even as she threw her arms around his neck. "What do you think you're doing?"

"Amazing. You can look all prim and tidy even when you're naked and ravished." He dropped a kiss on her mouth, a little slow, a little sweet, a little bit of tongue. "I haven't forgotten the second part of my plans for the evening."

"The second...oh." For once, she was able to follow one of his lightning mood changes and understand. Rafe wanted to distract her. He didn't want her worrying about the Kellys and the unholy mess her life was in.

Oh, yes. He was a good man. The least she could do was play along. She moistened her lips. "The part that takes place upstairs, you mean?"

"In my bed." He sounded thoroughly satisfied with the idea.

"As long as you've given up on the part involving—Rafe," she said firmly when he started walking, "you are not going to carry me up all those stairs."

"Want to bet?"

Rafe was very good with distractions. After losing the bet, Charlie didn't think about the Kellys or anything else for quite some time. But afterward she lay in his bed with his arm thrown loosely over her waist, holding her in place. His breath was warm against the side of her head, the tempo smooth and shallow with sleep.

But sleep was nowhere to be found for Charlie. She lay quietly in his arms for a very long time, staring dry-eyed at the darkness.

Eleven

Rafe was not a morning person. He didn't bound cheerfully out of bed at the crack of dawn, and didn't approve of those who did. Normally, though, especially near the end of a project, he woke up early whether he wanted to or not, his mind buzzing as it automatically picked up where he'd left off the night before.

He definitely wanted to pick up where he'd left off last night. But when he reached for Charlie, she wasn't there.

A sharp pang cleared the last traces of sleep. His eyes opened. Damn. He wished…a glance at the clock had him raising his eyebrows. It was three minutes after ten o'clock.

That explained why she wasn't beside him, he supposed. But he didn't like it. He'd wanted her there when he woke up. Scowling, he threw back the covers and padded, naked, down the hall to the bathroom.

She could have woken him up, couldn't she? If she'd gotten tired of waiting for him to wake up, she could have given him a shake. Or roused him in other, more pleasant ways.

Obviously she hadn't wanted to.

Rafe was in a thoroughly bad mood by the time he stepped under the shower. He'd thought last night was pretty special. Mind-bogglingly wonderful, in fact. Maybe she hadn't. That thought pinched at him in a place deep inside, the same place the fear had come from the first time he'd made love with Charlie.

His anger deflated in one slow exhalation. He put his hands on the side of the shower stall and leaned under the spray, not liking himself very much.

Maybe she'd wanted him there in the morning, too—that first morning, after their first time together. Maybe she'd been as crazy in love with him five months ago as he was with her right now.

Water continued to pound down on his shoulders and back. Rafe stood motionless. Dumbfounded. Just how long had he been falling in love without noticing? And what was he supposed to do about it?

His brain failed to come up with any suggestions. At last he shut off the water and shook his head, sending drops flying. This changed things. Explained things, too. No wonder he'd been so confused.

Are you using the woman to get the baby...or the baby to get the woman? Neither one is likely to work.

Rafe heaved an exasperated sigh. Damn. His father had known what was going on before he did. Grant Connelly had been right, too, in his annoyingly cryptic way. A man didn't use the ones he loved.

If she had been in love with him, even a little bit, he had hurt her badly when he climbed out of her bed and ran for cover.

Feeling like scum, Rafe grabbed a towel and rubbed himself dry, then went through the rest of his morning ritual. It was a wonder she'd slept with him again, he thought as he drew a razor along his jaw. Or maybe not. The razor paused. Why would a woman with Charlie's defenses give him a second chance?

He'd been ready to back off last night. *She'd* seduced *him.* Admittedly it hadn't taken much, but... Damned complicated woman. Grimly he finished shaving and rinsed the razor. The only explanations he could come up with for her change of mind didn't make him happy. If she hadn't cared deeply before, then she hadn't been badly hurt. Going for a second round might not have seemed too much to risk.

He didn't like that explanation because it meant he was the only one in love at the moment, but it could be worse. At least he would still have a chance to change her mind and her heart. It was the other possibility that had his jaw tight as he left the bathroom.

Maybe she'd cared too much and he'd killed her love, so now it didn't matter if she went to bed with him or not. He couldn't hurt her again because she didn't care at all.

The thought made him feel hollow and scared. He wanted to go downstairs and shake her and make her tell him how she felt, but he had enough sense left to know how well *that* would work. So he pulled on his jeans slowly, trying to figure out how to get a woman who never told him anything to tell him how she felt about him.

He was zipping his jeans when the smell reached him—yeasty, fragrant. Bread baking? And wasn't the scent of cinnamon mixed with it?

Cinnamon rolls. Charlie was making cinnamon rolls.

A woman might lose her head and have sex with a man she didn't care about—but she wouldn't bake him cinnamon rolls the next day.

Rafe didn't bother to grab a shirt on his way out of the bedroom.

"I had no idea you found cinnamon such an aphrodisiac."

"Absolutely. My reaction didn't have a thing to do with the fact that you're not wearing a thing beneath that robe.

But if you keep licking the crumbs off your lip that way, I'll have to demonstrate the power of cinnamon and yeast on my libido again.''

They were sitting on the couch, devouring the cinnamon rolls. She'd been taking them out of the oven when he came downstairs, which had struck him as perfect timing. He'd offered to thank her for the rolls. Since his hands had been inside her robe at the time, she'd taken his meaning. "A simple verbal thank-you would be sufficient," she'd told him politely without making the least objection to what he was doing.

"I do intend to express my appreciation orally," he'd assured her, lifting her onto the kitchen table and nudging her legs apart. "But not with words."

"I—oh, my. I didn't...I had no idea you liked... cinnamon rolls—" She'd gasped, her hands clenching in his hair. His mouth had been on her inner thigh by then. "S-so much."

Rafe smiled now, enjoying the memory and the moment. He loved looking at Charlie like this, all rumpled and glowing. She did tuck her tongue back in her mouth, but the sidelong glance she gave him was distinctly speculative. "You're considering going back for seconds? Already?"

"I might be able to handle another cinnamon roll, too."

She laughed, but shook her head. "We'd better not. We've lost most of the morning already."

Rafe nodded regretfully. At that moment only one thing seemed more important than making love to Charlie— keeping her safe. Which meant stopping the Kellys. Which meant he'd better get to work.

"Before you get lost in your programming," she said, rising and picking up their plates, "I had a couple of questions. That is, if it really is all right for me to work on this with you."

"It's more than all right," he said quietly. "I want your help."

She smiled, shy and pleased, and headed for the kitchen

with their dirty dishes. He smiled, too, as he followed her, amused by her incurable tidiness.

"I can't help with the actual programing, obviously," she said as she loaded the dishwasher. "So I've been going over the list of material stored in that partition."

"We've been over the list more than once." He poured the last of the coffee in his mug, sipped and made a face. It was cold.

"I assumed you had, but sometimes connections only become visible when material is sorted or classified in a particular way. At any rate, that type of thing is my strong point, so that seemed the best tack for me to take."

"Makes sense. Here, have one more." He added his cup to the dishwasher, then stuck in the empty carafe and got the machine running. When he turned around she was smiling that secretive smile of hers. "What?" he said, annoyed.

"You're cute when you're being domestic."

Cute. Great. So were teddy bears. He headed for the stairs. "So how have you organized the list?"

"First I'm eliminating everything that might be available elsewhere. They wouldn't have gone to this much trouble if they could get hold of whatever they're after somewhere else. I've been going over the corporate items first, of course." As they started up the stairs she added, "As I understand it, you, your father and the head of the computer department are the only ones who can access the partition."

"Theoretically true. In practice, Dad can never remember the protocol, which is rather involved. Mickey Tenjo—he's the corporate computer guru—and I are the only ones who really use it."

"Dix said you had an arrangement with the corporation that lets you store your own material in the partitioned area."

"Yeah." He glanced wistfully at the bedroom, but turned in at the office. "Security isn't Mickey's bailiwick, so it's a decent exchange. I get a secure off-site location for backups of some of my own sensitive material. They get an ultrasecure location for their most confidential stuff."

"I'll need you to look over this, then." She handed him a neatly printed list. "These are your files on the partition. I need to know if any of them are available elsewhere."

"They all are," he answered absently as he sat in front of his computer and hit the power switch. "They're copies of programs I've written for various clients, and related files. Obviously the client has at least one copy of the program."

"Oh. I guess they wouldn't be likely prospects, then. Although..."

"What?"

"Well, this one." She tapped the file named Altinst. "The précis says this is an encryption program. There are five of those listed, but this is the only one where the client isn't mentioned in the précis."

"That particular client was especially security-mad. Didn't want any copies of the program anywhere. I have to keep one so I can do updates, of course, but in deference to their paranoia I..." His voice drifted off. He frowned.

"What is it?"

"This may be just a coincidence, but...the client was The Rosemere Institute in Altaria."

"Rafe." Her hand closed around his wrist. "That's the kind of coincidence we've been looking for. Altaria has to be the key, doesn't it? The Kellys tried to have your brother assassinated—"

"We don't know it was the Kellys who tried to have Daniel killed. We know someone did, but the only solid link to the Kellys is Angie." And Charlie was the link to her. He drummed his fingers, thinking. "I don't see a motive. The Institute is involved in cancer research. What possible interest could the Kellys have in cancer research?"

"Maybe that's a front. Maybe this Institute is really doing something else."

"Hey." He grinned. "I just learned something else about you. You like spy thrillers."

"Don't joke. We need to find out for sure what this Institute is up to."

His fingers drummed again. Charlie was right—this was the only significant connection they'd found, and he'd be an idiot to ignore it just because it didn't make sense. "I'll call Daniel and ask him to check things out at his end. He's the king. They have to tell him what's going on."

She looked down, then away. The twist to her mouth was rueful. "Yes. Call your brother the king."

"I don't like the way you said that." He used his knuckles beneath her chin to tilt her face to him. "You prejudiced against royalty?"

A tiny head shake. "Never mind. Call Daniel, and I'll take a shower and get dressed."

Daniel wasn't an easy man to reach these days, but Rafe had his private number, which usually meant he only had to go through one intermediary. Gregor Paulus, the stiff and annoying personal assistant Daniel had inherited along with the throne, often answered the phone.

This time, though, Rafe lucked out and got his brother right away. "Hello?"

The protocol experts apparently hadn't had any better luck getting Daniel to change his telephone habits than their mother had. "I hope you didn't strain something," Rafe said solicitously.

"What are you talking about?"

"Answering your own phone like that. I know you're not used to doing things for yourself anymore. Probably have people around helping you get dressed, cut your meat, take a bath—"

Daniel's response was pungent and profane. Rafe grinned. His big brother was having a hard time adjusting to all the formal rigmarole that was so much a part of his new life. He figured he had a brotherly duty to be as annoying as possible and give Daniel a chance to blow off some steam.

"You didn't call just to make me mad," Daniel said after he'd expressed himself. "What's up?"

Rafe told him. Daniel was silent a moment. "I don't see a connection, either, but it's too much of a coincidence to ignore. I'll check with the scientists at the Institute and get back to you."

"Good enough. So, how's Erin?"

"Beautiful." A softness came into Daniel's voice when he spoke of his bride. "I hear you're thinking of taking the plunge, too."

"I'm working on it." Rafe frowned, still uneasy about the expression on Charlie's face when she referred to "your brother the king." There was something going on in that tricky mind of hers. "She's stubborn."

Daniel started to give him some big-brotherly advice. Fortunately, the intercom buzzed and Rafe was able to interrupt. "Got to go. Someone's here."

The identity of his visitor surprised him, though it probably shouldn't have. "Mom," he said, leaning forward to kiss her cheek. "Come in and warm up. Your nose is red."

Emma Connelly, née Rosemere, had never fully adjusted to the cold autumns and freezing winters of her adopted city. "You're not supposed to tell a woman her nose is red. Say, rather, that my cheeks are flushed."

"I never can remember all those female rules," he said sadly.

She pulled off her gloves and patted her son's cheek. "Brat. You remember exactly as much as you want to. Why are you running around without a shirt in this weather?"

"I'm building up my manly endurance," he said, moving behind her to help her off with her coat. "Once I get used to going shirtless in a heated apartment I'll try bathing in any icy fjord."

"Chicago has many amenities, but I don't think icy

fjords are among them. And that was a foolish question, wasn't it? You're living with a lovely young woman now. I suppose I should be glad you were wearing pants when you came to the door.''

"Ah…" To his dismay, his cheeks heated. He turned to hang up the coat he'd taken from her.

"I've embarrassed you. Good. A mother likes to be able to do that now and then. Where is Charlotte?"

"Upstairs." He couldn't hear the shower, so she was probably getting dressed. With luck his mother would assume she was in the office working rather than cleaning up after a bout of hot sex. "Can I get you something? I could heat up some water for tea."

"No, thank you, dear. I can't stay long. I just dropped by to meet Charlotte."

"Mom, you know Charlie."

"That's right, you like to call her Charlie, don't you? I wonder which she prefers? I'll have to ask her. I know her as my husband's assistant, not as the woman you want to marry. The woman who's carrying my grandchild, although, owing to the situation she's in, some people believe it's my husband's child."

His eyebrows lifted. "You in a hurry? You've taken the gloves off pretty quickly."

This time it was her cheeks that flushed. "I didn't come here to fight."

"Maybe you could give me a hint about why you did come here, then."

"I'm worried about you." Nervous or agitated, she moved farther into the room. "I've always tried not to be an interfering parent. Your father does enough of that for both of us," she added dryly. "And I'm not judging your Charlie harshly, truly I'm not. The problem is that I don't know her well enough to have an opinion at all. I don't know anything about her—except that Grant likes her, she's pregnant with your child and she connived with Angie

Donahue to let the Kellys do something to the computers at the corporation.''

''You might trust Dad's judgment,'' he said quietly. ''And mine. I like her, too.''

''But where is she from? What are her people like?'' She turned to face him. ''And is that all you feel for her? You like her?''

''Actually, I'm crazy in love with her. But I like her, too.''

His mother didn't say anything for a long moment. Then she sighed. ''Oh, my.''

He shook his head. ''I'm going to have to quit trying to predict your reactions. Oddly enough, I thought you'd be happy to hear that, considering I'm going to marry her.''

''She's agreed, then?''

''No. But I'm making progress.'' She was in his bed now. That had to be progress, but he didn't think he'd go into that with his mother.

''How does she feel about you?''

''I'm not sure,'' he said curtly. ''Look, you want to sit down and make yourself comfortable while you grill me?''

''I'm sorry. I am being a pain, aren't I?'' Instead of sitting she came closer and did one of those mother-things, smoothing his hair off his forehead. ''I can't seem to help myself. I'm going to say one more thing, then I promise I'll stop pushing. I hope you won't take this the wrong way, but...Grant said that he thinks she came from a rather poor background. Poor as in impoverished,'' she added quickly. ''I'm not concerned about her social standing.''

He had his doubts about that. His mother had done her best to adopt the democratic outlook of her husband's country, but she'd been born and raised a princess. ''What are you concerned about, then?''

''Disparate backgrounds put a strain on a marriage. A woman who grew up lacking material comforts could easily become caught up in the Cinderella fantasy. I just want you to be sure she isn't more enchanted by the Prince Charming aspects of marrying you than she is by you.''

He had to smile. ''That has to be the most tactful way possible of asking if she's marrying me for my money.''

''Is she?''

Charlie's words came back to haunt him: *You're a fool to want to marry a woman who's more interested in what you own than what you are.* She hadn't meant it, he reminded himself. She'd been striking back at him for what she thought he meant. ''Since she's laboring under the impression she isn't going to marry me at all, I think it's safe to conclude she hasn't mistaken me for Prince Charming. Or Daddy Warbucks.''

She smiled. ''All right. I promised I'd let the subject drop, and I am.''

''Good.'' He put an arm around her shoulder. He'd gotten through that pretty well, he thought. ''Now come sit down and tell me what a bad son I am for not coming to see you lately.'' Some internal radar had his head turning. He smiled. ''Charlie. Look who's here.''

She was coming down the stairs, looking pretty and neat in a loose-fitting wool dress in a dusky green. The white collar added a scholarly touch that suited her, but her hair was all curly and damp from her shower. And the wool was stretched over the bulge of her stomach in a way that made him smile.

Charlie smiled, too, as she came down the stairs, but it was that terribly polite smile of hers. She was manning the barricades, prepared to repel enemy attack—courteously.

''It's good to see you again, Mrs. Connelly,'' she said as she reached the bottom of the stairs.

''Make it Emma, please.'' His mother moved towards her, holding out both hands. ''Otherwise, if my son has his way and the two of you do marry, we'll be calling each other Mrs. Connelly and confusing everyone.''

''Emma,'' Charlie repeated dutifully, allowing his mother to take her hands. ''I'm not...'' Her breath huffed out suddenly, and she grimaced. "This is horribly awkward. I want to apologize for all the trouble I've caused your family."

Emma Connelly didn't treat apologies as a matter of form. She studied Charlie's face a moment. "Yes, I believe you mean that." She gave Charlotte's hands a squeeze and dropped them, smiling. "Apology accepted. Now, I was just telling Rafe I really can't stay. I only stopped by to give him a hard time, and make sure you knew about the party on Thursday."

She blinked. "What party?"

"It's just a family get-together—casual, in deference to Rafe's preferences. Drinks and dinner followed by birthday cake and baby pictures. I couldn't resist having some kind of party. Rafe's been out of town on his last two birthdays."

"Mom has a thing about birthday parties," Rafe explained. "I should have known she wouldn't let me turn thirty-four in peace."

Charlie lifted her eyebrows. "You'll be thirty-four next Thursday? I'm only twenty-six. I think you're too old for me."

"Nonsense. Everyone knows women mature faster than men. We're about even now." Rafe was encouraged. Charlie had loosened up enough with his mother to tease him. He was about to encourage some female bonding by making a chauvinistic comment—nothing united women faster than having a male to abuse—when the phone rang.

It was a former client, panicking over a minor glitch. Rafe listened, explained that he wouldn't be able to fly out immediately, and still managed to hear pretty much everything his mother and his lover said to each other. They were being very polite. Charlie's stiffness didn't surprise him, but he'd expected his mother to do better. She was normally very good at putting people at their ease.

When his mother started gently probing Charlie about her family, Rafe decided he'd better end the call. Before he could, Charlie turned the conversation neatly on its axis by asking Emma about Rafe's family.

"There's something I'm curious about," she said. "Rafe's brother is the new king of Altaria. Doesn't that mean Rafe is—well, a prince?"

Rafe winced at the echo of his talk with his mother about Prince Charming.

Emma looked uncomfortable. "Not in American eyes."

"As far as Altaria is concerned, though, he would be a prince?"

"Yes, in Altaria he would be. He's a long way from inheriting the throne, however."

"Of course." Charlie looked unhappy. "I see."

Aha. Rafe disconnected at last. His mother would take Charlie's reaction the wrong way, but he knew what it meant—and what her "your brother the king" expression had meant earlier. Charlie was playing snob on his behalf. She'd decided she didn't measure up socially.

He wasn't about to let her get away with that nonsense, but the phone rang again before he could tackle that job. "Hello," he snapped.

"Bad day?" Luke's voice said dryly.

"It's had its up and downs. What's up?"

Luke's news was good, but his timing sucked. Charlie had obviously listened in, because as soon as he disconnected she asked him what was going on.

"Nothing important," he said easily.

"You were talking to Luke and you mentioned my name, so it has something to do with my situation. I'm entitled to know."

She wouldn't thank him for blurting it out now. He tried to dodge. "I'll tell you later. Now, about that birthday party, Mom—"

His mother picked that moment to take sides. "Rafe, you shouldn't keep things to yourself that involve Charlotte."

He gave up. "Good news, Charlie. You don't have to worry about being arrested. Your warrant has been revoked."

Nausea rose, stomach to throat. Charlie swallowed and walked Emma Connelly to the door with Rafe, smiling pleasantly. She'd almost made it. In another few moments Mrs. Connelly would be gone...and then there would be just Rafe to deal with.

Rafe. Who had told his mother he was in love with her.

Somehow she'd managed not to give herself away, but she was too miserable to congratulate herself on her acting ability.

Charlie hadn't meant to eavesdrop. Some trick of acoustics in the high-ceilinged apartment had carried the voices to her clearly at the top of the stairs, and she'd taken a quick step back out of sight. At first it had been a cowardly urge to retreat until Rafe's mother had gone. Then she'd heard what they were saying.

She rested a hand on the turmoil of her stomach and breathed carefully as Rafe helped his mother on with her coat. The easy, ingrained courtesy of the act seemed symbolic of all that stood between them.

Rafe hadn't had to check books out of the library to know that napkins went in your lap, which fork to use, how to write a thank-you note. Of course, he probably didn't know the proper protocol for visiting a family member in prison. She was one up on him there.

Oh, Rafe. She rubbed her stomach. Had he meant it? Was it possible that he was really in love with her? He might have just wanted his mother to believe that. It had never occurred to Charlie that he might feel something more than friendly lust for her. The idea was astonishing. Wonderful. Terrifying.

She needed time, she thought desperately. Somehow she had to slow things down. Everything was happening too quickly. She couldn't deal with it. Time was the answer, time to plan, to adjust, to understand what was best for both of them, what she could reasonably hope for.

Oh, but reasonably, rationally, there was so little hope. Even if he'd meant what he said…her whole body felt dizzy and strange at the thought. But it wouldn't really be *her* he was in love with. There was too much he didn't know.

His mother was worried about him. Well, she should be, Charlie thought bitterly. And just think how much more Emma Connelly would worry if she knew the warrant that had just been dismissed wasn't the first one that had been issued with Charlie's name on it.

Rafe shut the door and turned. "Now, what's bothering you?"

"Nothing. It was kind of your mother to make sure I was invited to your birthday party."

"Yeah." His eyes were slightly narrowed as if he was studying her. "She's a great lady, but she didn't exactly shine today. I think you make her nervous."

"Me?" That was so absurd she dismissed it immediately. "Rafe, I don't think I should go to the party."

"Why not?" he demanded. "If you claim you'll feel out of place—"

"Well, I will." Desperate for distraction, she began stacking the scattered sheets of the newspaper. "She said this was a family affair. I'm not family."

"Close enough. Let's get one thing straight. You are not going to use my accidental connection to royalty as an excuse not to marry me."

She blinked. "I don't know what you mean."

"I mean that we're in America, this is the twenty-first century and I don't want to hear any nonsense about how different our backgrounds are. Because you don't mean backgrounds, you mean social standing. And that's crap. You can mix and mingle with anyone. You wouldn't have been such a great executive assistant if you hadn't been able to handle the rich and the snobby."

His compliment warmed her. And made it hard to argue. "Your family isn't snobby," she said weakly.

"No, they're not. Though my mother did inhale a lot of noblesse oblige during childhood, she does her best not to let it influence her now. And the rest of us don't give a hoot in hell about social standing. Charlie." He came to her then, smiling that beautiful smile of his and cupped her shoulders in his warm hands. "I want you there. I want to celebrate my birthday with you."

Her heart was beating too fast and her resolve was melting even faster. "I—I don't have anything to wear."

"Okay. We'll go shopping."

Twelve

"You were very patient," Charlie said as she dumped two sacks on the couch.

"I was a saint." Rafe didn't bother to drop his three sacks. He collapsed in the big purple chair with them still in his hands. "You've got the stamina of an ox. Never has a woman fought so hard to avoid spending a man's money, but once you surrendered, you shopped like there was no tomorrow."

Her brow puckering, Charlie looked at the department store bags with dismay. "I didn't realize… I shouldn't have let you talk me into buying so much."

"You needed maternity clothes," he said for the one hundred twenty-fourth time that afternoon.

"I'll take some of it back. That black dress— I don't need a cocktail dress, for heaven's sake. And I certainly don't need four pairs of maternity slacks."

He looked at her and shook his head. "If you put me to the trouble of running around and buying back a bunch of

stuff you've returned, I'm going to be mad." He let the
shopping bags fall from his hands and stretched, legs out,
arms over his head. "You know, Charlie, if I didn't know
better I'd think you didn't have a single gold-digging bone
in your body."

She bit her lip. Maybe she should have spent twice as
much of his money instead of protesting every time he
handed her something else to try on. Maybe she ought to
be persuading him that she was after his money, so he
wouldn't care too much and wouldn't be hurt. She wanted
so badly to do the right thing...if only she knew what the
right thing was.

"I'm plenty greedy," she said lightly. "I'm going to
take everything upstairs and gloat over it before I put it
away." She bent to pick up the sacks he'd dropped.

His arm snaked around her waist and dumped her over
the arm of the chair and into his lap. "Yeah, you're a
greedy woman." He nuzzled her hair. "That's okay. I
loved the way your eyes lit up over that silk dress. You
can thank me now," he added. "With words if you must,
but if you'll cast your mind back to this morning and the
way I thanked you for those cinnamon rolls, it might give
you a clue what I'd prefer."

She was already fighting a smile. Putting her hands on
his chest, she tried to ignore the spreading warmth and the
interesting bulge beneath her rump. "Are you trying to
make me feel like a kept woman? Buy me a few trinkets
and I'm supposed to fall on my back and show my appreciation?"

"Your back, my lap, your knees—whatever works. As
for making you a kept woman..." Banter died out of his
voice and his eyes, leaving them serious and soft. "That's
what I have in mind, Charlie. Keeping you."

Her mouth went dry. "Keeping the baby, you mean."

"That's what I thought at first, so I can't blame you for
believing it now." His hands slid up her sides, pausing just

below her breasts. "I was a little slow catching on. Did you overhear what my mother said this morning?"

"I—I don't—what do you mean?"

"You're a lousy liar, did you know that? You can keep a secret forever, but you can't lie worth beans. That's reassuring. I'm talking about Mom spouting all that crap about Cinderella and Prince Charming. You heard her, didn't you?"

Her mind went blank. She licked her lips nervously.

He nodded. "That's what I thought. Let me take this point by point. First there's that Cinderella nonsense." His fingers slid up a fraction, so that the sides of his hands pushed against the soft bottoms of her breasts. "You're about as far from Cinderella as a woman can be. If some prince tried to sweep you off your feet and carry you off to his castle, you'd turn up your nose, say no thank you very politely, and go right back to organizing your ugly stepsisters until the family business showed a profit. You are dead set on making it on your own, Charlie. Maybe you need to prove you can. The last thing you want is to have anything handed to you. My money is an obstacle to our marriage, not an incentive."

How did he know? How *could* he know her so well?

"Still nothing to say?" He smiled. "Okay. I'll move on to the important part. You heard what I said to Mom, too, didn't you?"

Panic rose, a great, dark beast pushing words out every which way. "Don't say it, Rafe. I can't hear that right now."

His expression darkened. "Tough. I don't just want the baby, Charlie I want you. I—"

Acting without thinking, she pressed her lips to his. The kiss was frantic, a little sloppy. He responded anyway, his hands tightening on her ribs. She opened her mouth, inviting more, craving the haste and the hunger. Her pulse throbbed in her throat as the liquid heat spread.

He tore his mouth away, catching her face in both hands.

His eyes were stormy, his mouth hard. "Damn you," he said, but then he kissed her again, harder, his tongue thrusting deeply inside.

Relief made her tender. It must be relief, this soft aching that sent her hands roaming gently over him, searching the places she knew he liked to be touched. Oh, such sweet, delicious relief....

"Let me," she whispered as she dotted kisses along his jaw. "Let me make love to you this time." She ran her hands along his shoulders, loving the firm, round shape of the muscles, then drew her hands down along his chest. Slowly she began unbuttoning his shirt.

He leaned back in the chair, his eyes hot and unsmiling, watching her as she unfastened his shirt and opened it.

Rafe's chest was perfect—not too lean, not too brawny, with just a sprinkling of hair right in the center. Charlie had always secretly loved the look of a tight male butt, but Rafe's chest had converted her. She ran her hands over him, enjoying the way his muscles quivered beneath her touch. Then she leaned forward and tickled one small, flat nipple with her tongue.

He sucked in his breath. Encouraged, she laid down a path with her mouth, testing the texture of the skin along his collarbone, comparing that to the smooth skin of his stomach just above his belt buckle.

His stomach muscles clenched. Hard.

She slipped from his lap, kneeling in front of him and watching his face. Slowly she unfastened his belt. Then the snap of his jeans. A muscle jumped in his jaw. As if they were connected, her heart jumped, too, pounding harder. Next, his zipper. She went very slowly there, drawing out the movement, brushing her fingers along the hard length beneath.

His eyes closed as his breath shuddered out. "You're killing me. You know that, don't you?"

"No, you have to live a little longer." She'd never set out to deliberately arouse a man this way. It was exciting.

Intoxicating. She freed him from his jeans and licked her lips.

He groaned. "I hope you mean that."

Her mouth curved up. Sweetness pulsed between her legs. Oh, yes, this was quite delicious. She leaned forward and tasted him.

He made a wonderfully guttural noise that aroused her spirit of experimentation. She ran her tongue up, down, and around, then settled in to see how wild she could make him. He didn't let her enjoy herself for long, though. His hands slid beneath her arms and lifted, and a second later she was sprawled across him, mouth to mouth.

He shoved her dress up, groaning when he discovered her panty hose but sliding his hand between her legs anyway. She jolted, the shock of his touch so strong it almost tipped her over the edge. His fingers moved back and forth, and the friction made her crazy. Moaning, she tore her mouth away from his and pushed back to stand on shaky legs in front of him—and slowly, very slowly, pull her panty hose down.

Oh, he liked that. His gaze followed her hands, and his whole body looked tense enough to shatter. With her panty hose gone she climbed back in his lap, straddling him, letting her skirt ride up. Reaching beneath, she guided him inside her.

The heat, the fullness—the sense of being filled by *him*—overcame her, and her breath hissed out between her lips. He wound one hand in her hair and tugged her face to his. Mouths joined, they began to move—slowly at first as she adjusted to him and the position, then faster. Until he seized her hips in an iron grip and took over, thrusting up into her over and over. He put his hand near the spot where they were joined and brushed her with his fingers. Her vision dimmed and her body bucked with the force of climax.

He was right behind her.

Dishrag-limp, she rested against him, her head on his

shoulder, aftershocks making her inner muscles clench every so often. Her mind floated, distant and unimportant.

"I survived," Rafe murmured close to her ear. "Amazing. But if you keep doing *that* I'll have to start all over again, and that will surely kill me."

"Doing what?" Another little aftershock rippled through her.

"That."

Oh. Her inside muscles. "I can't help it."

"You're blushing," he pointed out.

"I can't help that, either."

"The female mind never fails to astonish me. Why that would make you blush after you..." Mercifully, he didn't finish the sentence. Instead he pressed a kiss to her cheek and for a few moments they drifted together in dreamy silence. Finally she stirred. He helped her lift slightly, then rearrange herself so that she sat sideways across his lap, cuddled up to his chest.

After a moment she said, "I wonder how long the phone has been ringing."

"What phone?"

She giggled and put her hand over her mouth. She *never* giggled.

"I'm getting to you." He shifted her gently so he could stand and fasten his jeans. "Pretty soon you'll be running wild, scattering the newspaper all over the floor and forgetting to make the bed. God knows where it will end."

His voice was lazy, amused. He was smiling but he wasn't looking at her. "Now, where's the phone?" He glanced around as if it might wave at him.

"On the base unit on the hutch." She'd put it where it belonged during a brief fit of tidying before they left to go shopping. *It isn't that he's avoiding meeting my eyes,* she told herself. He was looking for the phone, that was all.

Even as he started toward it, the answering machine picked up. Charlie heard a voice she recognized from her years of working for Grant—Daniel Connelly, the oldest son. The king of Altaria. "Why the hell do you have such a long delay set before your blasted machine picks up?" his voice demanded from the speaker on the base unit. "Never mind. Rafe, call me right away. It's—"

Rafe picked up the phone. "I'm here. What is it?"

Though she only heard one side of the conversation, that was enough to destroy the languor from their lovemaking. She scrambled to her feet, dimly aware of the stickiness between her thighs, the chill rising from the floor beneath her bare feet. But that wasn't as important as whatever Daniel was telling Rafe. She watched his expression go from shock to stunned horror to dead-serious determination, and waited with growing fear.

At last he disconnected. "Dear God."

She took a quick step toward him. "What did he tell you?"

"Your hunch was right. They want the encryption program for the Institute. Get your shoes on." He moved quickly, scooping up her panty hose, tossing them at her and heading for the coat closet.

"But what do they want it for?" She scrambled into the panty hose as quickly as possible. "And where are we going?"

"To see my father and get that damned encryption program off the hard drive."

"But I thought they couldn't get to it." She stepped into her shoes.

"Nothing is foolproof enough. We can't take *any* chances, not with what's at stake."

What was at stake? "You said something about a virus. Why would the Kellys spend so much effort on a computer virus?"

"Not a computer virus." He handed her coat to her, his expression wholly grim. "A human one. Those ivory-tower innocents at the Institute are trying to create a genetically engineered virus that will target cancer cells in humans. Along the way they accidentally created another type of virus altogether. One that *causes* cancer—fast-growing and lethal. It's highly contagious and vectored through the air.''

Horror chilled her so powerfully that goose bumps popped out on her arms and legs. ''Dear God. You're thinking it could be used as a—a biological weapon.''

''Oh, yes. And the Kellys want to sell it to the highest bidder.''

Thirteen

Rafe had worked hard before. For the four days following that phone call from his brother, he worked like a man driven by demons.

With reason. Charlotte wasn't an overly imaginative woman, but she had to work to shut out horrific visions of what might happen if the wrong people got their hands on the killer virus. There were biological weapons aplenty already in existence, of course, but this virus was apparently a huge leap ahead of them because of its ease of delivery and transmission.

The scientists at Rosemere Institute weren't irresponsible. They'd been horrified when they realized what they'd created, and the Institute's director had immediately informed the former king. King Thomas had ordered all samples of the virus destroyed, along with every description of it and how it had been created. But according to the director, a well-funded lab could recreate the virus if they had access to the Institute's database. Much of the research, therefore, had been encrypted, using Rafe's program.

As soon as they'd told Grant Connelly about the virus, he'd summoned Luke Starwind. After some discussion, they had agreed with Daniel that the U.S. government shouldn't be brought in right now. The fewer people who knew of the existence of the virus, the better. If they had any reason to think the data was in imminent danger of falling into the Kellys' hands, that would have to change, of course. But for now only Rafe, Grant, Luke, Daniel and Charlie knew the truth.

Daniel had increased security at the Institute itself, Luke Starwind had stepped up his investigation, and Rafe had removed the program from the Connelly computers. He'd burned it onto a CD, but she didn't know what he'd done with that CD. Nor did she want to know.

Charlie had never felt so far out of her depth. She couldn't do anything to help Rafe; after the second day even Dix hadn't been able to help. Rafe wasn't sleeping enough. She wasn't sure he'd slept at all last night, but there was nothing she could do. So she cleaned and organized and cooked and worried. Rafe's apartment had probably never looked so neat.

Not that he'd noticed. He was so immersed in his work she wasn't sure he knew she was around, except late at night, when he finally came to bed. Then he made love to her with a quiet ferocity that overwhelmed her every bit as much as learning about the virus had—but in a far different way.

He scarcely spoke to her the rest of the time.

That was all right, she told herself as she pulled her hair back in a quick ponytail. She didn't expect him to lavish attention on her at a time like this, with so much depending on him. If he was silent and grim, he had reason. She wasn't going to jump to any self-centered conclusions. His mood had nothing to do with her and the words she hadn't let him speak.

She hadn't hurt him. Surely he didn't care enough to be really hurt, did he? If he did…if he'd meant what he said to his mother—

Charlie reached out blindly, grabbing a lipstick at random. As soon as she'd sleeked a little color over her lips she hurried down the stairs.

Dix was waiting for her in his favorite cap, a black leather jacket, black slacks and turtleneck. He lifted his pierced eyebrow. "Never saw a woman get ready that fast."

"I'm stir-crazy," she said lightly. "I haven't been outside this apartment in days." Four of them, to be precise. Ever since she and Rafe had gone to Connelly Corporation to erase the encryption program. Absently she smoothed the rusty-red sweater she was wearing. He'd bought it for her.

"You left a note for Rafe?"

She nodded. She'd told him she was going shopping, too, of course, but getting Rafe's attention when he was this far into his programming world wasn't easy. Dix had suggested she leave him a note in case he forgot what she'd said.

"Okay, let's go. But I'm warning you," he said with a ferocious frown. "Two stores. That's my limit."

Three stores later, he was not happy. "So what's wrong with that sweater?" he demanded.

"It just isn't right." Nothing had been right. Hastily she refolded the sweater and put it back in the stack. "It isn't personal enough."

"You want personal, buy him underwear," Dix muttered.

She bit her lip and looked around. She didn't even know what to look at next. Maybe something for the kitchen? He liked to cook. Where was the housewares department?

Oh, what was she going to do—buy him a blender? Frustration tightened her mouth. She turned back to the sweaters again.

"If you don't make up your mind soon, I'm gonna carry you out of here. I'm tired of the way that saleslady's looking at me."

"Maybe she isn't a Cubs fan." She knew what he meant, though. The woman had kept Dix in view the whole time. It reminded Charlie of the way clerks used to watch her, many years ago. Because she remembered how horrid that had felt, she started moving. "We'll try the next floor up. Maybe there's some techno marvel he doesn't have."

Dix fell into step beside her, but shook his head. "You said you didn't have much to spend. Everything in this place costs plenty. The techno toys sure won't be cheap."

She stopped and scowled at him. "What do you suggest, then? You've known Rafe a long time. Don't you have any ideas?"

"What do I know about this sort of thing? Buy him a CD. He likes music."

"Great idea," she muttered, moving ahead. "A lovely, thoughtful birthday present for a man like Rafe. A CD. Maybe we should go to the discount store and check out the blue light special."

He looked disgusted. "You think the value of a gift is what it costs?"

"No. No, I don't, but if I can't find something special, something personal, I can at least give him something that costs more than $19.95." Suddenly, to her horror, her eyes filled. "I don't know what to get him. How can I not know what to get him?"

"Whoa." Dix eyed her with alarm, then grabbed her arm and pulled her toward the escalator. "Time out. We're going to that ritzy tea shop on the second floor. We'll sit at one of those dinky tables and drink water that tastes like boiled rocks and let the hostess worry about me snagging the silverware. And you'll probably tell me what's wrong, whether I want you to or not."

"I'm sorry," she said, almost stumbling to keep up with him. "I don't usually...it's the stress. I'm not a crier."

"That's good, 'cause I do not *do* crying females. You get yourself dried up quick," he ordered her. And he continued to chide her and drag her gently along until they were sitting at "one of those dinky tables" in the tea shop.

"There," Dix said with relief after the waitress set cups of steaming tea in front of them. "Drink your boiled rocks. You'll be better in a minute."

She sniffed and smiled. Dix's technique was bracing but effective.

"Thank God you aren't one of those women who have to tell a man every little personal detail. I hate relationship talks. I don't want to hear about how you and Rafe aren't communicating."

"Okay." She sipped the tea. It was a soothing blend of chamomile and some other herb.

Dix frowned at his cup. "He's a good man," he said abruptly.

"Yes, he is," she agreed, a wave of sadness putting her dry eyes in danger. "He's wonderful."

"He doesn't get the money thing, though. He never thinks about whether a person has money or not—it doesn't matter to him. But when you've grown up rough, you can't ever see things quite that way." He met her eyes steadily. "I think you know what I mean."

She rubbed her thumb over the handle of the cup, looking down at the pale amber brew. "I didn't think it showed anymore."

"Mostly it doesn't. But I saw you at the dive where you were working. You talked fancy, but you knew how to handle yourself. You know the streets."

Her mouth curved in bitter humor. "I didn't ever work them, if you're wondering."

"Didn't figure you had. Too prissy by half." He took a sip of his tea, made a face and put it down. "God knows how you can stand this stuff. You ever wonder how someone like me got to be friends with someone like Rafe?"

"It has crossed my mind."

"I hacked into one of his systems when I was younger and a lot dumber, left a snotty note—to prove I could, you know. Just like the idiots who get caught hacking into SAC or the DOD. He tracked me down so fast it was embarrassing, thanked me for pointing out a flaw in his program, told me he'd kick my butt if I ever did it again, and we started talking. I'd still be a two-bit hacker if it weren't for him. Now I'm a consultant." He grinned. "Pays a lot better than leaving snotty notes."

"That sounds like Rafe." She smoothed her thumb along the handle of her teacup. "He gets mad, but he doesn't judge."

"Exactly. Now, I don't know what's wrong between the two of you—and don't you go telling me, either." He held up a hand as if she'd been about to burst into confession. "But I figure whatever isn't working, it's your fault."

"Gee, thanks." Miffed but amused by his unabashedly partisan support, she asked, "You don't think you might be a bit biased?"

"Of course I am. But after watching you today, I have to think part of the problem is the money thing. He has it, always had. You don't, never did. But like I said, there isn't a problem on his side. He doesn't think that way. So the problem's with you."

"In your limited way, you're right." She sighed. "But that doesn't give me a clue how to deal with it. And I don't think this is the time for me to—to bring any of that up, anyway, not with the pressure he's under."

"I don't know what's going on. I know something has changed, and this deal with the Kellys has gotten a lot hairier. I also know that whatever's wrong with the two of you is eating at him. I want you to fix it. You aren't quite stupid enough to be blaming yourself for not being born rich—"

"Another compliment. I'm overwhelmed."

"So I figure there's something else. Like maybe you're

blaming yourself for something you did because you didn't have money.''

She stiffened. That was entirely too close to the mark.

''So what you have to do is tell him about it. Even if it's bad. Especially if it's bad. If you don't level with him, you're not dealing straight and things will go right on being messed up. Damn,'' he said, pushing his chair back. ''I can't take this place another minute. Let's get out of here.''

She tried to pay for the tea. He gave her a disgusted look and told her not to insult him. After that, neither of them said much. She let him steer her out of the store and down the street to an El station.

Dix was right. Obnoxious and biased, but right. She'd been telling herself this wasn't the time, that Rafe had too much on his mind for her to bring up painful subjects, but that was a cop-out. She'd been protecting herself, not him, hanging on to the last remnants of a dream that wouldn't die, no matter how often she told herself it had.

She had to tell him everything. Today. The thought made her half-sick with dread, but she'd deal with that. ''Wait a minute,'' she said, noticing at last that they weren't going in the right direction. ''Where are you taking me?''

''To see my cousin. You wanted suggestions on what to get Rafe. I've got one.''

''I knew you were a hacker. I had no idea you were a con artist, too.'' Charlie punched the elevator button in the lobby of Rafe's building. ''I don't know how I let you talk me into this.''

''Didn't have to. You talked yourself into it just fine.'' Dix was grinning smugly as they stepped into the elevator.

''You caught me in a weak moment. I—'' A little pink tongue licked her face and she went all mushy inside. ''Yes, sweetie, we're almost there. You want to get down and run around, don't you?''

''He might have something else he needs to do.''

''He just did that.''

"Puppies do it a lot. You'll have to put newspapers down."

The elevator doors opened. She stepped out, cuddling Rafe's present close. "I shouldn't have done this. What made me think Rafe would want a puppy peeing all over? He doesn't have time to take care of a dog right now!" She stopped. Had she had some stupid idea at the back of her mind that if Rafe accepted a mongrel puppy, he'd accept her, too, as she really was? "I've lost my mind. We have to take him back."

"Keep moving." A hand at her back encouraged that. "You're not taking that puppy back. You're nuts about him. And my cousin has probably left the neighborhood by now. He's no dummy."

Dix's cousin had had three of the little darlings left. All were guaranteed to have no pedigree whatsoever. The one Charlie had lost her heart to looked like a cross between a beagle and a few dozen other breeds. He was a dirty white all over except for a big, brown patch over one eye.

"Rafe's going to think I've lost my mind," she muttered, trying to juggle an excited puppy in one arm while she pulled out the key. "You just don't give someone a puppy unless you're sure he wants a dog. It's thoughtless. I don't even know if his lease allows pets."

"You said someone else in the building had a dog." Dix took the key from her, stuck it in the top lock and started working his way down. "He'll like the puppy. Tell him you'll take care of it, train it."

"I don't know how." And what if she wasn't around? What if he didn't *want* her around after he realized the woman he might be in love with was a fabrication, that the prim and correct Ms. Masters didn't really exist?

Charlie's heart was pounding when the door swung open—pushed from the inside.

Rafe stood there glowering at her. "Where the hell have you been?"

Dix put down the puppy kibble he'd brought. "I'm out of here."

"Coward," Charlotte muttered, but he was already in the elevator.

Rafe's furious gaze zeroed in on the wiggly bundle in her arms. "Good God. What in the world are you doing with *that?*"

Oh, yes, this was a great idea. Rafe was obviously thrilled. Tears stung her eyes. "Here," she snapped, thrusting the puppy at Rafe and shoving past him. "And happy birthday."

Rafe shut the door and refastened all the locks. He was still so mad he wanted to choke her. Some of that mad, he admitted, had nothing to do with today and everything to do with what had happened four days ago, and the pain that didn't seem to grow any less as time went on.

Charlie didn't want his love. His body, yeah. She liked it just fine. His protection—she was reluctant about that, but she'd accept it for now. But not his love.

Turning, he absently began running one soft, floppy ear through his fingers. The puppy wriggled in delight and insisted on licking his chin.

Reluctantly he smiled. Ugly little runt.

Happy birthday, she'd said. His practical, logical Charlie had gotten him a puppy for his birthday? An ugly little mongrel puppy, which, from the look of things, wouldn't stay little for long. It was such a foolish thing to do. So unlike her. He looked up from his adoring present.

Charlie was speeding around the room, looking for something to clean or straighten. She had to settle for plumping some pillows. She'd already done everything else.

Had he really seen tears in her eyes? "I was scared," he said abruptly.

She didn't look at him. Those pillows were desperately in need of fluffing, all right. "I told you I was going shopping. I left you a note."

"Yeah, well...after you left I got a phone call from Elena Connelly—formerly Detective Delgado of the SIU. She'd been keeping us posted as much as she can on what the police discover."

Her busy hands stilled and she faced him, still holding one blue pillow. "There's news?"

"You know they thought the hit man was Rocky Palermo."

"The Kelly enforcer. Yes. Have they—has he gotten away from their surveillance?"

"No." His muscles tightened up again, making him sound curt. "They've had a tip from an informant. Word is that the Kellys hired another hit man after Palermo missed. This one's not part of the organization. He's got quite a reputation. According to Elena, he makes Palermo look like one of the losing contestants on Amateur Hour."

She stood frozen, no expression at all on her face, that pillow hugged tight to her chest. "They think this other hit man is the one after me?"

He nodded. "Why didn't you take a cell phone?"

"I didn't think of it. You didn't, either."

No, he hadn't. He'd been too focused on his work and had barely paid attention when she said she was going shopping. And he'd been furious with himself when he realized he'd let her and Dix leave without having any way to get in touch with them.

A small pink tongue recalled his attention. He looked down and idly played with the soft pad of one paw, then shook his head. Either the pup was deformed or he was going to be one big dog. "Thumbs."

"What?"

"I'm going to call him Thumbs." He scratched behind the puppy's ears, sending him into a frenzy of pleasure, and tried to make sense of a woman who didn't want his love, but gave him a puppy for his birthday. Her timing couldn't have been much worse. He glanced up. "Thank you for the birthday present, Charlie."

She moved closer, smiling hesitantly. "Dix bought the puppy food. He said that's his present."

Dix had also cleared out immediately. Smart man. Rafe sighed and held out the puppy. "We're going to talk, but not now. Here. You'd better put him in the kitchen with some newspapers."

She took the puppy, but her smile vanished. "Sure. I'll take care of him, don't worry. It was a dumb idea, Rafe. I'm sorry. I don't know what—"

"Charlie." He laid his fingertips on her lips. "Hush. The puppy's great. I can't stay and get acquainted right now, though. I've got to go. I should have already left, but—" But he hadn't wanted to. Not until he knew she was okay.

Abruptly he turned and headed for the door.

"Why? Where are you going?"

"I finished the program. I need to install it on-site."

Rafe leaned his head back and let the cabbie worry about traffic and everything else. His head buzzed with programming language, street sounds and the look in Charlie's eyes when he'd said he would call the puppy Thumbs. He was too tired to make sense of any of it, too keyed up to doze off. But he was done. Somehow he'd crammed at least a week's worth of work into four days. The program was installed, and every test he'd been able to run told him it would work.

And Charlie was waiting back at the apartment. With Thumbs. A tired grin touched his mouth. Crazy woman.

Crazy him, for being so crazy about her.

The ghost of a grin vanished as the cab pulled up in front of his apartment building.

Picking up the mail on his way was automatic. Sorting through it in the elevator was equally mindless. Until he hit the long white envelope addressed to Charlotte Masters...from Brad Fowler, Deer Lodge Prison, Bridleton, Connecticut.

Fury seared away fatigue. He stared at the return address,

his mouth tight, jealousy and pain pumping through him with every heartbeat.

This time she would give him some answers.

Charlie gave the pepper mill a few more twists, then stirred the simmering soup. She'd wanted something that would keep if necessary. Rafe might want to sleep before eating—heaven knew he'd done little enough of that lately, and he'd be up tonight if the hacker accessed the Connelly system. She could watch the alarm thingee he'd rigged and wake him if—

She heard the front door open and close. "I'm in the kitchen," she called. Thumbs was curled up near her feet. She had to step over him to put up the pepper mill. "Is everything ready?" she asked, turning around.

He stood in the doorway. His eyes were shadowed, drawn with fatigue, hard. Without saying a word he came into the kitchen and slapped an envelope down on the counter beside her.

It was a letter from Brad. Sickly she realized the time for truth had arrived. Her hands were shaky when she reached for the dishtowel. "You want to know why I never told you about him, I suppose."

"Damned right I do." The glitter in his eyes scared her a little. "Is *he* the reason you cooperated with the Kellys?"

"Yes. I—"

"I knew it." He began to pace. "By God, I knew it. When I saw that bundle of letters you kept I wondered...but you're carrying *my* child. You're sleeping with me. And you're writing some other man—a convict, for God's sake!"

Her eyes closed. Oh, this ought to be funny. Rafe thought Brad was another man. But she couldn't find a grain of amusement to lighten the dread coiled in the pit of her stomach. "He's—"

"He's history, that's what he is! Starting right now, he's your past. I can't believe you gave him this address. No one's supposed to know where you are. No one. And you wrote this convict, this criminal lover of yours—''

''Your family knows where I am!''

''What does that have to do with anything? If you're going to tell me this guy is like family to you, I don't want to hear it!''

''He's not like family, he *is* family!''

He stopped.

She swallowed. ''Brad is my brother.''

An odd, blank look settled over his face. ''You don't have a brother.''

''I—I lied on my application at Connelly's.''

Abruptly he turned and walked out of the kitchen.

Slowly she followed.

Rafe was sitting on the big, apricot-colored couch, his legs sprawled, rubbing his face with both hands. When she stopped in front of him, he spoke without looking up. ''His last name is Fowler, not Masters.''

''My parents didn't marry until I was three, just before Brad was born. He carries our father's name. I don't.''

''I see.'' His voice was carefully level. ''And he works for the Kellys? That's why you did as they asked?''

''No! God, no, it wasn't like that. Th-they sent me the tip of his little finger.''

His head jerked up.

She swallowed bile. ''It was waiting for me in an express mailer the night their man contacted me.''

''I'm sorry.'' His voice was muffled. ''I'm sorry I accused you of…but I don't understand. How could you not tell me you had a brother? I knew you had secrets, but I never thought…how could you not tell me about something as important as that?''

''Because that wasn't the only thing I lied about.''

He dropped his hands between his knees and shook his head slowly, like a swimmer in deep water. ''You have more brothers? A sister or two? Your parents are alive and well and living in Florida under an assumed name?''

"No more brothers, or family of any sort. My parents were killed in a rollover when I was seventeen, just as I said on my application. I persuaded the court to let me have custody of Brad—he's three years younger than me—and I shouldn't have. I made a lousy guardian. He was in trouble all the time. When he was nineteen, he was arrested for selling drugs."

He said nothing at all.

Her hands were clenched together so tightly her fingers were starting to tingle. She had to finish now, get it all out in the open, or she'd lose her nerve. "I was arrested once, too."

"Yeah, I know. For helping your father with the numbers operation he was running. They dropped the charges, probably because you were a juvenile and your father said he'd made you do it."

Shock froze her. She couldn't speak, move, think.

His eyes widened. "That's it? That's your deep, dark secret? Jesus!" He collapsed against the back of the couch, his legs stretched out, slumped so deeply his head rested against the back of the couch. "All this time I've been waiting to hear something horrible—that you turned tricks or plotted armed robberies or something."

"You knew?" Her voice was high and unfamiliar. "How did you—how *could* you know?"

"I dug into your background some when you went into hiding. And don't go getting all huffy about it. I had to. How do you think I turned up your mother's social security number?"

"But juvenile records are *sealed*."

He gave her a get-real look. "Yeah. So?"

"How could you have found about my record and not known about my brother?"

"I saw a record of your arrest. For some reason the cops didn't put 'P.S. She has a brother named Brad' at the bottom of it." His eyes closed wearily. "I can't believe it. With all your defenses I thought there had to be something really horrible in your past. Turns out you couldn't even trust me enough to tell me you had a brother and got into a little trouble when you were sixteen.''

''It was more than a little trouble,'' she said stiffly. ''And my father...''

His eyes opened. ''I guess it must have seemed like great big trouble at the time. And your father did end up serving some time, a few months, anyway. Sit down, will you? My neck's getting a crick in it from looking up.''

Dizzy, confused and vaguely offended by his easy dismissal of a past that shamed her, she sat on the edge of the couch.

He looped an arm around her and pulled her up against him. She lay there stiffly, unable to relax. He didn't seem to notice. ''That's better. Now, tell me about your father. How did he wind up running numbers? Had he always leaned toward the crooked end of things?''

''N-no.'' She was so badly off-balance she didn't know what she was saying. ''At heart he was a wanderer. He never could settle in one job, one place. But he was also a family man, so he took us with him.'' A bittersweet smile touched the corners of her mouth. ''I'd lived in seventeen cities by the time I was twelve. Big cities, mostly. He wasn't much for small towns or the country.''

''He took you with him, at least. He must have loved you.''

''Yes.'' That was both comfort and a source of guilt. Her parents *had* loved her and Brad. And she'd loved them. Her grief had been hard and painful when they were killed. But the truth was that she'd resented them, too, and there had been times when she'd secretly wished her mother would stop following her father from city to city and dragging them along.

But her mother had never really grown up, no more than her father had. A sweet woman sometimes bewildered by the turns her life took, she'd never lost faith that her husband would someday make everything right. Jack Fowler had been a cheerful drifter, always convinced he would hit it big one day if he could just be in the right place at the right time. San Diego, L.A., Galveston, New Orleans, New York City, Boston. They were in Mobile for a few months, but that job hadn't worked out—they never did—then down to Miami.

"I was twelve the first time he strayed from the straight and narrow. He was working for a wealthy man in Miami. Odd jobs, mostly. Handyman work and filling in for the chauffeur. He wanted to give me and Brad a big Christmas that year, so he—he stole from his employer." The shame and guilt swept over her again. "We had a splendid Christmas, all right. A huge tree, lots of presents. The next day his employer—who, as it turned out, had ties to some unsavory people—fired Dad. Then he had him beaten. We left the city as soon as he was well enough to travel."

"That ought to have scared him into good behavior."

"For a while it did." Gradually she began to relax into his warmth. "Over the next few years he worked as a blackjack dealer, a horse trainer—that didn't last long, since he knew nothing about horses. He was a stand-up comedian and a sanitation worker, among other things. The only other time he dabbled in crime was when he tried his hand at running numbers. He was caught pretty quickly. He wasn't a very successful crook." Her smile was easier this time, if rueful. "His one real talent was forging whatever credentials he needed to get a job."

"A marketable skill, but not much use in the long run."

She slid him a sideways glance. "I used what I'd learned from him about that when I applied for the job with your father. Most of my work history is fabricated."

"Hmm. Sounds like Dad needs to tighten his personnel procedures." Rafe settled a little more, his legs outstretched. "How did you keep the Kellys from making good on their threat to your brother? He's alive and writing to you, so you must have done something."

"When I was shot at, I figured all deals were off. I

couldn't trust them not to do something to Brad—take off another finger, or worse—as a lesson to me. And I didn't want to die, or to let them get away with everything. So I made a deal with Lieutenant Johnson. In return for my testimony he pulled some strings and got Brad secretly transferred to another prison under another name. He's still carried on the records at Deer Lodge Prison, but his mail goes to the warden, who forwards it to wherever he is now. Just as his letters to me go to Deer Lodge Prison first, so the postmark and everything will make it look like he's still there.''

Rafe didn't say anything, and for a few minutes she didn't, either. It felt strange to have everything out in the open. He hadn't been shocked. He'd already known about her arrest, and that still made no sense to her. How could he have known and not spoken of it? How could it matter so little to him?

He'd been hurt, though. She'd hurt him by not trusting him with the truth. ''I've always been…intimidated by your family,'' she said shyly. ''Not by the money—no, to be honest, that's part of it. But only part. Your family—they're all so strong and honorable. None of them would just drift, doing whatever came easiest. There always seemed such a huge gulf between us. And I've always admired your father so much. I…''

She turned her head to look at him. And had to smile.

His eyes were closed. His mouth hung open, and his breath sighed in and out evenly. He was sound asleep.

Charlie eased away. Much as she would have liked to stay snuggled up to him, she was afraid she'd doze off, too. While she hadn't been running on stubborn instead of sleep as much as he had, she hadn't been sleeping well, either. And someone had to stay awake in case the ''hacker alarm'' went off.

She spread a throw over him and left him to his dreams, feeling the sweet, sharp bite of hope as her own dreams stirred stubbornly to life once more.

* * *

Eighteen blocks away, in a pleasant if generic hotel room, Edwin Tefteller hummed along with Pachelbel's *Canon* as he packed his favorite silencer in the specially designed briefcase that held his SIG Sauer.

He was looking forward to the evening.

It was always pleasant to discover that one's instincts, based on planning and research, had been correct. The brother had indeed proven to be the key to locating his target a second time. The parolee who handled the warden's mail at Deer Lodge Prison had been admirably quick about passing Edwin the return address on the letter Ms. Masters had sent her brother.

If truth be told, he was a bit disappointed in her. She'd seemed staunchly independent. Yet she'd gone to roost with her lover, abrogating her responsibility for her own welfare. But he was charitable enough to allow that women were hampered by their biology. Given an opportunity to depend on a male, particularly one who had impregnated them, they inevitably took it. Even the admirable Ms. Masters.

He'd been watching the apartment for the last three days while gathering information on Rafe Connelly. His target had stayed sensibly inside until today. He had very nearly had her three times while she wandered the stores with her companion, but each time someone else had moved to ruin the shot. When the two of them had gone into the El station, he'd come back to the hotel.

It was quite possible to kill someone on the subway or in a crowd, but there were a great many variables involved. Edwin preferred to control the setting whenever possible. That wouldn't be difficult with this job.

His suitcase was already packed. He went through the room, using a hotel towel to wipe down every surface he might possibly have touched. He doubted very much the police would dust this room for prints, but he hadn't risen to the top of his profession by leaving things to chance.

If there had been time, he would have arranged to rent

an office in the building across from Rafe Connelly's apartment and wait for his shot. The windows were large—an easy shot for a marksman of his skill. The only difficulty would have been acquiring the office. His employer, however, was applying a great deal of pressure. Franklin Kelly wanted the job done quickly. Edwin had decided to accommodate his employer's wishes.

Besides, there was a certain intimacy to killing someone in her home. Edwin enjoyed it when he was the last thing his targets saw. He wouldn't jeopardize a job or himself to indulge that preference, of course, but in this case his personal tastes fit neatly with the most efficient way of concluding the job. He was good with locks.

Finished with his final tidying, he folded the towel and put it with the other dirty linen. He didn't expect to have a problem with Rafe Connelly. The man was a computer programmer, not a martial arts expert. Not that Edwin was underestimating him. Connelly was fifteen years younger than Edwin and quite fit—the information Edwin had gathered indicated he indulged in such daredevil sports as hang-gliding. A great foolishness, in Edwin's opinion, but it indicated a degree of athletic prowess, the ability to react quickly and a certain disregard for personal safety.

No, he wouldn't underestimate Rafe Connelly, Edwin thought as he closed his hotel door behind him for the last time. Nor would he give the man time to indulge his penchant for taking risks. He would shoot Connelly first, then Ms. Masters.

Fourteen

Someone was shaking him. Rafe stirred and waved a hand, trying to shove them away.

"Rafe! Rafe, you have to wake up. The alarm sounded. The hacker is accessing the computers *now!*"

He was off the couch before his eyes fully opened. He took the stairs three at a time. "Get hold of Luke!" he called as he sat at his computer.

Dammit, Broderton had signed on early tonight. Rafe had planned to be at the corporate offices at the usual time the man hacked into the system—there was a measurable lag doing it this way, even with the fastest connection.

But his connection was damned fast. And his program—"Yes!" he cried. "Got him. I'm in."

"Already?" Charlie's incredulous voice came from the doorway.

"Broderton is good," Rafe said tersely as his fingers flew over the keyboard. "So's his worm. But mine is better."

Data was coming in. Rafe had it routed to the Connelly mainframe, but he had complete access to that. As long as Broderton kept the connection open… Rafe called up a file, and whistled under his breath. "Did you call Luke?"

"I'm ringing him now. He hasn't answered yet."

"As soon as you get him—"

"Luke? This is Charlotte. Rafe installed his program this afternoon and he's got an open connection to the hacker right now. He wants to talk to you."

He waved the phone away. "Tell him to get his butt over here. I'm into the Kellys' computer, not just Broderton's PC. And I'm getting plenty from it."

Just before 3:00 a.m. Broderton signed off and the connection was lost. Rafe, Charlie and Luke didn't know that, though. They were in a warehouse on the south side of Chicago that was owned by Connelly Corporation.

Grant Connelly was with them. He held a portable scanning device. "This is the one," he said tersely, and stepped back.

Luke had a crowbar the night watchman had found for them before Grant sent him away. He used it to pry open the large packing crate whose bar code matched the one given in one of the files Rafe had downloaded from the Kelly computers. The wood creaked and parted with a loud crack.

Charlie's job—holding the flashlight—wasn't really necessary, but she'd flatly refused to stay at the apartment while the men flexed their muscles and located what the Kellys had gone to such trouble to smuggle into the country. According to the file Rafe had found, this shipment of lace imported by Connelly's from an Altarian manufacturer contained something not listed on the cargo manifest.

It took Luke and Rafe together to tip the huge crate over on its side. The two of them dug through the contents with a complete disregard for the worth of the fine lace, ripping open the flat, heavy packages one at a time.

"Here it is." Rafe crouched beside the upended crate, holding a small, padded box. He opened it.

Inside were five innocuous-looking CDs.

"That's it?" Grant looked dubious. "Are you sure?"

"They didn't go to all this trouble to smuggle contraband music into the U.S.," Rafe said dryly. "But I'll check it just to be sure."

He'd brought his laptop with him, with the encryption program loaded on it. Half an hour before they'd left the apartment, Dix had shown up, handed Rafe the CD that contained the program and waited while Rafe loaded it on his laptop. He'd taken the CD with him when he left—all without asking a single question.

Charlie waited tensely while Rafe inserted one of the CDs. First he looked at a file without running the program that would remove the encryption; the screen showed garbage. Then he opened the file again, using the encryption program. "This is it, all right," he said grimly. "Not that I can understand one word in ten, but it's related to DNA encoding." He handed the CD to Luke. "The police will need these."

The police would not be told what was on the CDs, or about the copy of the encryption program that Rafe was even now erasing from his laptop's drive. But the existence of the CDs would tie the Kellys to a smuggling operation that had cost one man his life.

Grant frowned. "I'm not convinced we should let those CDs out of our sight. If they fall into the wrong hands...you said yourself any code can be broken."

"Eventually, yes. But this is one hell of a good code." Rafe's grin was tired but cocky. "Besides, these five CDs cover only a fraction of the Institute's database. Genetic research generates incredibly massive amounts of data. The Kellys have been smuggling these things out for some time—what we have here is a drop in the bucket, nowhere near enough for anyone to use to replicate the virus."

"The police can definitely use these to build their case

against the Kellys,'' Luke said. ''If you're sure they can't be used—''

''I'm sure.'' Abruptly Rafe pushed to his feet. ''Dad, it's time to get your friend the judge on the phone. The police will need to move fast to confiscate the Kellys' computer. The quicker and quieter a search warrant is issued, the better.''

Grant nodded grimly. ''I'll see what I can do.''

Grant drove them back to Rafe's apartment. Luke was to take the CDs—and the story of how they found them—straight to the police. Charlie and Rafe could expect a visit from the cops soon after that.

Rafe slept most of the way. Charlie, too, was exhausted—too tired to make conversation, but too wired to doze off.

Was it really almost over? Once the Kellys had been arrested, would they call off their hired killer—or be more determined than ever to see her dead for her part in their downfall? And Rafe—would they try to take vengeance on him?

She gripped his hand tightly the whole way.

Rafe woke just as they pulled up in front of his apartment building. He exchanged a few low-voiced words with his father, then he and Charlie climbed out.

The night was no more quiet than any other in this part of Chicago. Pedestrians were nonexistent, but cars cruised the street even at this hour. The air was knife-edge cold.

Rafe's arms were warm when he wrapped her in them. ''We've got a lot of talking to do,'' he murmured close to her ear. ''But I'm about to fall over, I'm so tired.''

''It can wait.''

''Falling over?''

She giggled, punch-drunk all of sudden with exhaustion and success. Rafe had done it. He'd stopped the Kellys. Somehow they'd find a way to make sure he didn't pay a terrible price for having taken on the mob. "I'm hoping you'll postpone falling down until you're near the bed."

"Bed," he said longingly. "I wish I could promise to do what I'm supposed to once we get there, but..."

"What you're supposed to do is sleep. We'll have time for other activities later."

"Other activities." He grinned. "I love it when you talk prissy."

Arms looped around each others' waists, they wobbled into the lobby like a pair of drunks. Rafe punched for the elevator, urging her to "talk prissy" some more. She giggled and he bent to nibble her neck in the elevator, pretending to be a great deal more turned on than was humanly possible at this point.

He unlocked the door. She went in first. "Uh-oh," she said. "Good thing we left the lights on or I would have stepped in it."

"Stepped in what?" Rafe asked.

"Looks like Thumbs got out of the kitchen. I don't know how. I could have sworn I had him barricaded in there." She sighed. "At least he didn't go on the rug."

"My fault, I'm afraid," said a soft tenor voice. And a round-faced man wearing glasses and a pleasant smile stepped out of the kitchen doorway. With casual ease he pointed the gun he held directly at Rafe—and stumbled.

Thumbs yelped. Something coughed. Rafe threw himself forward as Thumbs shot out from under the hit man's feet a split-second before Rafe collided with the man, taking him down. They rolled, Rafe's hand imprisoning the man's gun arm. Another coughing sound—oh, God, he had a silencer on his gun and was shooting!

Rafe shouted at her to get back. She danced over to the other side, away from the gun, looking around frantically for a weapon, any kind of weapon, but she'd tidied things up too well. There was nothing close by.

She wasn't needed. The scuffle was fierce but brief, and ended with Rafe sitting on the hit man's chest, pinning his arms at the wrists. His eyes had rolled back from a vicious series of punches.

"Get his gun," Rafe ordered.

Even half-conscious, the man was feebly trying to dislodge Rafe—and he'd held onto his long, wicked-looking gun. Charlie scrambled close and wrenched it from his grip. Once she did, she knelt beside him and put the barrel up to his temple.

He froze. "The trigger is extremely sensitive."

"Then you want to be extremely still. I'm scared, I'm shaking and the least little surprise might make my finger twitch."

He was wonderfully obedient.

Charlie held herself together while they waited for the beat cops to arrive. She kept her cool while they cuffed the hit man and read him his rights. More police arrived and she answered questions and more questions.

The hit man didn't speak at all except to mutter something about puppies and dog pee and planning. He looked quite bewildered as they took him away.

Even when Lieutenant Johnson arrived and she had to answer the same questions all over again, she held on to her composure by repeating silently that it was over, that the man who had almost killed Rafe and her was gone, and soon the cops would be gone, too. In spite of what she'd said to the hit man, she didn't start to shake until the lieutenant announced that they would have to go down to the station to finish making their statements.

Once she started, though, she couldn't seem to stop.

Rafe didn't exactly argue with the lieutenant. He just told him they weren't going anywhere. The lieutenant argued. Rafe put his arms around her and held on and ignored the man, who finally went away.

That's when she started crying.

Rafe looked alarmed. "Hey, Charlie, it's okay. Everything's all right now. You're just having a reaction to all the adrenaline your body didn't use. You're okay."

"I didn't—he didn't—" But the tears were coming harder and she couldn't get the words out. She wrapped her arms around him.

Rafe was priceless in many emergencies, but he was helpless with tears. He kept telling her she was all right— as if she didn't know that—and to stop crying, which was no help at all.

Finally she grabbed the front of his sweater in both hands. "I-I'll cry if I w-want to!" she choked out. "Don't t-tell me to stop! You were almost *k-killed* tonight because of *me* and I *love* you and I damned well d-deserve to cry!"

His eyes went wide. "You love me?"

She sniffed and sniffed again, but the tears seemed to have at last run their course. "Of course I do! Why else would I put up with a stubborn, sloppy man who falls asleep when I'm baring my soul? And who tries to push me around and doesn't understand that I don't have a clue how to belong in his world, but—"

He gave a loud yelp—which woke Thumbs, who'd dozed off sometime between the arrival of the police and their exit—and grabbed her and whirled her around.

"Are you crazy?" But she was laughing as they spun in a circle, her hands on his shoulders and her feet flying clear off the ground.

"Crazy about you." His voice went soft and full of wonder as he pulled her close. "Charlie. You love me."

She nodded and swallowed. "I couldn't let you say it to me before because I didn't think it was *me* you'd be saying it to. There was so much you didn't know about me...." She frowned. "At least I thought you didn't know."

"I'm going to hear about that for the next thirty or forty years, aren't I?" He smoothed the hair back from her face, his eyes tender and happy. "Charlie, I'm nuts about your prim-and-proper side—which isn't fake, you know. You really do get off on neatness. But I'm just as crazy about the wild, wanton woman you don't let out enough. The woman who does illogical things like get me a puppy for my birthday—a gift that saved both our lives.''

Her smile wobbled a bit. "It was so close. If Thumbs hadn't come out right then—''

"Life isn't horseshoes, so 'close' doesn't count. In case you didn't notice, I did not propose again. I'm not going to, either. You keep turning me down. I'm simply telling you that we're getting married as soon as possible. It's only reasonable, since you love me and all.''

She bit her lip to hold back her laughter. "Rafe.''

His gaze had drifted to her mouth with unmistakable interest. "Yeah?''

"You're forgetting something.''

He frowned. "A ring? I'll get you one, don't worry.''

She shook her head.

"The carrying-over-the-threshold bit comes later. No, I can't think of anything I've left out that needs doing at this point. Other than—''

She put her hand on his chest. "You're far too tired for that.''

"Want to bet?" And he kissed her. Long minutes later he lifted his head, smiled down into her eyes and said softly, "Charlie, I love you.''

And quietly, happily, she let go of those pesky dreams. It was easy to do. There would be other dreams to enjoy, different ones, but she didn't have to dream of love anymore. Now she had the real thing.

She had Rafe.

Epilogue

The day after Thanksgiving

The bride wore a sarong. It was blue and brief, and made no attempt to camouflage the swell of her belly. Her hair was loose and curly, ornamented only by the white orchid tucked behind one ear. After the ceremony she tossed several leis to the guests instead of a single bouquet.

The groom was more traditional. He wore a tux. When the dancing started, though, he lost the jacket and let the tie hang loose before leading his new wife onto the dance floor.

"You looked sexy in that tux," Charlie said, casting his discarded finery a wistful glance.

"It's too warm in here for a jacket." Rafe pulled her into his arms and started them moving to the music. The band was playing "Blue Hawaii." Three inches of snow covered the ground outside, but his folks had turned the heat up in the ballroom to accommodate the bride's bare shoulders.

"I'm comfortable."

"Yeah." He ran one hand down her hip and, reluctantly, back up to her waist. "You sure are."

She smiled a private smile that hinted she was thinking things she wouldn't tell. "You'd be nice and cool if you'd worn the loincloth."

Charlie had suggested the groom ought to wear a grass loincloth like the sword dancers. Rafe still wasn't sure she'd been kidding. "I've created a monster," he said, and held her closer.

Charlie looped both arms around his neck and tilted her head back. "So, what do you think of marriage so far?"

"It's already changing me. I never used to be turned on by married women." He showed her what he meant with a kiss, long and deep and lingering. *His*. She was his now in the eyes of man and God, and the knowledge made him eager to switch from vertical dancing to the horizontal sort.

Someone tapped on his shoulder. "We're all enjoying the show, but I'm a little concerned that you've forgotten to breathe."

Rafe lifted his head slowly, smiling down into Charlie's eyes. At some point the band had stopped playing. No one was dancing anymore. No, the idiots were all standing around, watching and chuckling. And Charlie was blushing. "Damn voyeurs. Go away, Dix."

"No, I'm going to dance with the bride and you're going to pretend to be civilized and go talk to your guests. Move over."

Reluctantly he moved to the side of the dance floor as the musicians started playing again. He'd have to dance with several of the other ladies present, and it wasn't as if he didn't like them and want to dance with them, but…

"I'm not offering a penny for those thoughts," his father said with a chuckle. "The way you're watching her it's a wonder she doesn't spontaneously combust."

Oh, but she did. Rafe grinned. "I can wait. I guess I'd better start doing my duty and dancing with as many family members as possible. Where's Grandmother?"

"Giving Catherine's new husband a test drive, as she put it. Said she'd never danced with a sheik before."

Oh, yes. He saw now—the erect old lady beaming at the dark young man. "Pity Daniel and Erin couldn't make it," he said, snagging a glass of champagne off the tray of a passing waiter.

"They sent their apologies. Between taking on the duties of ruling a country and getting ready for the upcoming coronation, Daniel's stretched pretty thin right now." Grant chuckled. "It will be a wonder if he makes it to the ceremony without committing murder. Gregor Paulus is driving him crazy. I suggested that firing the man was a more politically correct solution than choking him."

Daniel had more on his mind than his irritating assistant. Rafe's mood sobered. The Kellys had all been arrested. It was one of the biggest sweeps of gang bosses in recent years, and the police were convinced their case was tight.

That case had been much strengthened when the hit man Rafe had caught decided to testify against his former employers. Edwin Tefteller seemed much more concerned about the black mark on his reputation than with the prison term he faced. He was determined to set the record straight. The Kellys had apparently violated their agreement with the hit man by sending Palermo after Charlie the first time. From that breech of contract, the hit man believed, all his own ills had sprung.

But no one knew how the CDs had been made and smuggled out of Altaria in the first place—or where the rest of the CDs were, or how many there were. And as he'd said, no encryption program was fail-safe. If the CDs fell into the wrong hands, eventually they could be decoded. A lab might be able to reconstruct the steps to creating the killer virus.

Then there was the Kellys' enforcer, Rocky Palermo,

who had managed to lose his police tail and vanish. All in all, there were a lot of loose ends. And they were all scary.

His father's annoyed exclamation broke into Rafe's troubled thoughts. "What is that little hussy of mine up to now?"

Rafe followed his father's gaze. His youngest sister, Maggie, was more or less dragging Luke out on the dance floor. "Looks like she wants to dance," he said mildly, but uneasiness grew as he watched. The moment Luke stopped resisting Maggie's blandishments and drew her into his arms, the two moved together with a physical harmony Rafe recognized all too well. The attraction was obviously strong—and mutual.

"Luke's a good man," he said, reminding himself.

"He's too old for her," Grant growled.

"Maggie doesn't seem to think so." And that wasn't what worried Rafe. The differences the calendar registered were far less important than the ones experience had carved into his friend. Luke was a good man, yes. But the shadow on his soul was large and dark, and Rafe didn't want his irrepressible sister damaged by that darkness.

So he made a point of dancing with Maggie next. After that he snagged his grandmother, then his mother. Then someone tapped his shoulder just as he was about to take one of his sisters-in-law out on the floor.

"I hope you'll excuse me," Charlie said apologetically to Elena. "But I bribed the band to play this song. It's rather special to me, and I'd like to dance to it with Rafe."

"By all means," Elena said, smiling.

So Rafe danced his second dance with his wife to the sound of "Dream a Little Dream." Her eyes were glowing, her cheeks flushed with pleasure. And her mouth was turned up in that secret-loving smile of hers.

He held her a little closer, smiling himself. He could let her keep a few secrets…for now. He had a lifetime to learn them.

*   *   *   *   *

DYNASTIES: THE CONNELLYS *continues....*

Turn the page for a bonus look at what's in store for you in the next Connellys book— only from Silhouette Desire!

#1478 CHEROKEE MARRIAGE DARE
by Sheri WhiteFeather
December 2002

One

Maggie Connelly waited on Luke Starwind's doorstep. The Chicago wind blew bitter and brisk. She could feel the December air creeping up her spine like icy fingers. A warning, she thought. A prelude to danger.

Adjusting the grocery bags in her arms, she shifted her stance. Was she getting in over her head? Playing with fire?

No, she told herself. She had every right to get involved in her family's investigation. She needed to make a difference, to find closure. Her beloved grandfather was dead, and so was her dashing, handsome uncle. Their lives had been destroyed, and she needed to know why.

But her biggest stumbling block was Luke. She knew the former Green Beret would try to thwart her efforts.

Maggie tossed her head. Well, she had a surprise in store for him. She'd uncovered a valuable piece of evidence. And that was her ace in the hole, the card up her sleeve. He couldn't very well shut her out once she revealed the winning hand fate had dealt her.

Luke opened the door, but neither said a word.

Instead, their gazes locked.

Maggie took a deep breath, forcing oxygen into her lungs.

The man stood tall and powerfully built. Jet-black hair, combed away from his forehead, intensified the rawboned angles of his face. He possessed a commanding presence, his features strong and determined—high-cut cheekbones, a nose that might have suffered a long-healed break, an unrelenting jaw.

Luke was a jigsaw puzzle she'd yet to solve, each complicated piece of his personality as confusing as the next. Everything about him rattled her senses, and made her want to touch him. Not just his body, but also his heart.

His reclusive, shielded heart.

Did Luke know that he had a romantic side? A masculine warmth hidden beneath that stern, rugged exterior?

Maggie had asked him to dance at her brother's wedding reception, and now she could feel every gliding motion, every smooth sultry sway. He'd rubbed his cheek against her temple and whispered a Cherokee phrase, something that had made him draw her closer to his beating heart. She'd never been so tenderly aroused.

"What are you doing here?"

Instantly, Maggie snapped to attention. After that sensual dance, he'd avoided her like the plague, returning to his hard-boiled self.

But why? She wondered. Because she'd made him feel too much?

Refusing to be intimidated, she shoved the groceries at him. "I came to fix you dinner, Starwind. So be a gentleman, will ya?"

Flustered, he took the bags, nearly dropping one in the process.

Maggie bit back a satisfied smile. She'd managed to catch Mr. Tough Guy off guard. That, in itself, rang like a small victory.

He moved away from the door and she swept past him, curious to see his home.

She zeroed in on the kitchen and headed toward it, knowing Luke followed. He set the groceries on a tiled counter, and she familiarized herself with his spotless appliances and practical cookware.

Something inside her stirred—a wave of sadness—an urge to brighten his rough-hewn world. To make Mr. Tough Guy smile.

He frowned. And for an instant, she feared he'd just read her mind.

He leaned against a pantry-style cabinet, watching every move she made. Maggie unbuttoned her coat and told herself to relax. The man was a top-notch private investigator. It was his nature to study people and make analytical assessments. Plus, she thought, releasing the breath she'd been holding, he was attracted to her.

Their bodies had brushed seductively on the dance floor, their hearts had pounded to the same erotic rhythm. *A qua da nv do.* The Cherokee words swirled in her head. What did they mean? And why had he said them with such quiet longing?

Maggie hung her coat behind a straight-back chair in the connecting dining room. Luke's gaze roamed from her cashmere sweater to the tips of her Italian boots, then back up again.

"What's going on?" he asked. "What are you up to?"

"Nothing," she responded, a little too innocently. She wasn't ready to drop the bomb. First she would ply him with pasta. And a bottle of her favorite wine.

Luke crossed his arms. He wore jeans and a dark blue sweatshirt, attire much too casual for his unyielding posture. In his left ear, a tiny sterling hoop shone bright against dark skin. The earring defined the native in him, she thought. A man who remained close to his Cherokee roots.

She unloaded the groceries and realized he intended to

stay right where he was, staring at her while she prepared their meal.

"I'm surprised you know how to cook," he said.

She shot him a pointed look. "Very funny." Maggie knew how Luke perceived her. No one took her endeavors seriously.

She was the youngest daughter of one of the wealthiest, most powerful families in the country. Her elegant mother hailed from royalty, and her steely-eyed father had made his fortune in business, transforming a small company into a global corporation.

But Maggie had yet to earn the respect often associated with the Connelly name. The paparazzi deemed her a spoiled, jet-setting heiress. The tabloid pictures that circulated made her seem like nothing but a party girl. It was an image she couldn't seem to shake, no matter how hard she tried.

And while Maggie's personal life was dissected in gossip columns, Luke kept a tight rein on his.

Why was he so detached? She wondered. So cautious? Why would a handsome, successful, thirty-nine-year-old choose to protect his heart?

She didn't know much about Luke, but she'd done a little digging, asking anyone who knew him for information. And although she hadn't been able to unravel the mystery surrounding him, she'd learned a few unsettling facts. Luke had never been married or engaged. He didn't participate in meaningful relationships, and most people, including women, described him as guarded.

Maggie held his watchful gaze, searching for a flicker of happiness, a spark of joy. But his eyes seemed distant. Haunted, she thought, by undisclosed pain.

Could she make him happy? Could she hold him close and ease the tension from his brow?

Deep down, she wanted the chance to try. But she doubted he would welcome her efforts. Especially when she told him that she intended to help him with her family's investigation.

Lucas Starwind, she knew, wouldn't appreciate the Connellys' youngest daughter working by his side.

DYNASTIES: THE CONNELLYS

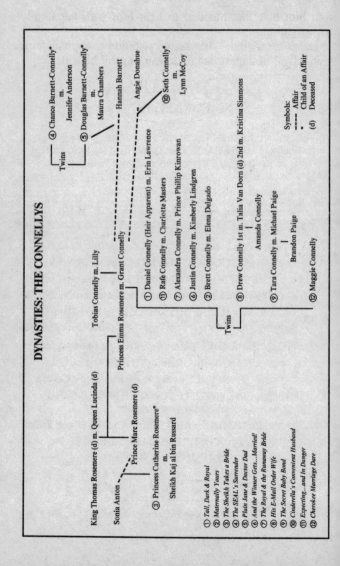

King Thomas Rosemere (d) m. Queen Lucinda (d)

Prince Marc Rosemere (d)

Sonia Anton

③ Princess Catherine Rosemere*
m.
Sheikh Kaj al bin Russard

Tobias Connelly m. Lilly

Princess Emma Rosemere m. Grant Connelly

④ Chance Barnett-Connelly*
m.
Jennifer Anderson

⑤ Douglas Barnett-Connelly*
m.
Maura Chambers

Twins

Hannah Barnett

Angie Donahue

⑩ Seth Connelly*
m.
Lynn McCoy

① Daniel Connelly (Heir Apparent) m. Erin Lawrence

⑪ Rafe Connelly m. Charlotte Masters

⑦ Alexandra Connelly m. Prince Phillip Kinrowan

⑥ Justin Connelly m. Kimberly Lindgren

② Brett Connelly m. Elena Delgado

⑧ Drew Connelly 1st m. Talia Van Dorn (d) 2nd m. Kristina Simmons

Amanda Connelly

⑨ Tara Connelly m. Michael Paige

Brandon Paige

⑫ Maggie Connelly

Twins

① *Tall, Dark & Royal*
② *Maternally Yours*
③ *The Sheikh Takes a Bride*
④ *The SEAL's Surrender*
⑤ *Plain Jane & Doctor Dad*
⑥ *And the Winner Gets...Married!*
⑦ *The Royal & the Runaway Bride*
⑧ *His E-Mail Order Wife*
⑨ *The Secret Baby Bond*
⑩ *Cinderella's Convenient Husband*
⑪ *Expecting...and In Danger*
⑫ *Cherokee Marriage Dare*

Symbols:
----- Affair
* Child of an Affair
(d) Deceased

Silhouette Desire

presents

DYNASTIES: THE CONNELLYS

A brand-new miniseries about the Connellys of Chicago,
a wealthy, powerful American family tied by blood to the
royal family of the island kingdom of Altaria.
They're wealthy, powerful and rocked by
scandal, betrayal...and passion!

Look for a whole year of glamorous and
utterly romantic tales in 2002:

Silhouette®

Where love comes alive™

Visit Silhouette at www.eHarlequin.com   SDDYN02

If you enjoyed what you just read,
then we've got an offer you can't resist!

Take 2 bestselling
love stories FREE!
Plus get a FREE surprise gift!

Clip this page and mail it to Silhouette Reader Service™

IN U.S.A.
3010 Walden Ave.
P.O. Box 1867
Buffalo, N.Y. 14240-1867

IN CANADA
P.O. Box 609
Fort Erie, Ontario
L2A 5X3

YES! Please send me 2 free Silhouette Desire® novels and my free surprise gift. After receiving them, if I don't wish to receive anymore, I can return the shipping statement marked cancel. If I don't cancel, I will receive 6 brand-new novels every month, before they're available in stores! In the U.S.A., bill me at the bargain price of $3.57 plus 25¢ shipping and handling per book and applicable sales tax, if any*. In Canada, bill me at the bargain price of $4.24 plus 25¢ shipping and handling per book and applicable taxes**. That's the complete price and a savings of at least 10% off the cover prices—what a great deal! I understand that accepting the 2 free books and gift places me under no obligation ever to buy any books. I can always return a shipment and cancel at any time. Even if I never buy another book from Silhouette, the 2 free books and gift are mine to keep forever.

225 SDN DNUP
326 SDN DNUQ

Name	(PLEASE PRINT)	
Address	Apt.#	
City	State/Prov.	Zip/Postal Code

* Terms and prices subject to change without notice. Sales tax applicable in N.Y.
** Canadian residents will be charged applicable provincial taxes and GST.
All orders subject to approval. Offer limited to one per household and not valid to
current Silhouette Desire® subscribers.
® are registered trademarks of Harlequin Books S.A., used under license.

DES02   ©1998 Harlequin Enterprises Limited

$ Saving Money $ Has Never Been This Easy!

Just fill out and send in this form from any October, November and December 2002 books and we will send you a coupon booklet worth a total savings of $20.00 off future purchases of Harlequin and Silhouette books in 2003.

Yes! It's that easy!

....

I accept your incredible offer!
Please send me a coupon booklet:

_____
Name (PLEASE PRINT)

_____
Address   Apt. #

_____
City   State/Prov.   Zip/Postal Code

In a typical month, how many
Harlequin and Silhouette novels do you read?

❑ 0-2   ❑ 3+

097KJKDNC7   097KJKDNDP

....

Please send this form to:
   In the U.S.: Harlequin Books, P.O. Box 9071, Buffalo, NY 14269-9071
   In Canada: Harlequin Books, P.O. Box 609, Fort Erie, Ontario L2A 5X3

Allow 4-6 weeks for delivery. Limit one coupon booklet per household. Must be postmarked no later than January 15, 2003.

HARLEQUIN®
Makes any time special®

Silhouette
Where love comes alive™

© 2002 Harlequin Enterprises Limited   PHQ402

October 2002
TAMING THE OUTLAW
#1465 by Cindy Gerard

Don't miss bestselling author
Cindy Gerard's exciting story about
a sexy cowboy's reunion with his
old flame—and the daughter he
didn't know he had!

November 2002
ALL IN THE GAME
#1471 by Barbara Boswell

In the latest tale by beloved
Desire author Barbara Boswell,
a feisty beauty joins her twin as a
reality game show contestant in an
island paradise…and comes face-to-
face with her teenage crush!

December 2002
A COWBOY & A GENTLEMAN
#1477 by Ann Major

Sparks fly when two fiery Texans are
brought together by matchmaking
relatives, in this dynamic story by
the ever-popular Ann Major.

MAN OF THE MONTH

Some men are made for lovin'—and you're sure to love
these three upcoming men of the month!

Available at your favorite retail outlet.

Where love comes alive™

Visit Silhouette at www.eHarlequin.com   SDMOM02Q4

Silhouette® Desire®

COMING NEXT MONTH

#1477 A COWBOY & A GENTLEMAN—Ann Major
Zoe Duke ran off to Greece to nurse her broken heart, and the last person she expected to come face-to-face with was her high school sweetheart—the irresistible Anthony. He had made love to and then betrayed her eight years before. But he was back, and though he still made her feverish with desire, could she trust him?

#1478 CHEROKEE MARRIAGE DARE—Sheri WhiteFeather
Dynasties: The Connellys
Never one to resist a challenge, feisty Maggie Connelly vowed to save tall, dark and brooding Luke Starwind's soul. In exchange, he had to promise to marry her—if she could rescue him from his demons. Maggie ached for Luke, and while he seemed determined to keep his distance from her, *she* was determined to break him down—one kiss at a time….

#1479 A YOUNGER MAN—Rochelle Alers
Veronica Johnson-Hamlin had escaped to her vacation home for some much-needed rest and relaxation. When her car got a flat tire, J. Kumi Walker, a gorgeous ex-marine ten years her junior, came to her aid. Veronica quickly discovered how much she and Kumi had in common—including a sizzling attraction. But would family problems and their age difference keep them apart?

#1480 ROYALLY PREGNANT—Barbara McCauley
Crown and Glory
Forced to do the bidding of terrorists in exchange for her grandmother's life, Emily Bridgewater staged an accident, faked amnesia and set out to seduce Prince Dylan Penwyck. But Emily hadn't counted on falling for her handsome target. Dylan was everything she wanted…and the father of her unborn child. She only hoped he would forgive her once he learned the truth.

#1481 HER TEXAN TEMPTATION—Shirley Rogers
Upon her father's death, Mary Beth Adams returned to Texas to take over her family's ranch. She would do anything to keep the ranch—even accept help from cowboy Deke McCall, the man she'd always secretly loved. There was an undeniable attraction between them, but Mary Beth wanted more than just Deke's body—she wanted his heart!

#1482 BABY & THE BEAST—Laura Wright
When millionaire recluse Michael Wulf rescued a very pregnant Isabella Spencer from a blizzard, he didn't expect to have to deliver her baby, Emily. Days passed, and Michael's frozen heart began to thaw in response to lovely Isabella's hot kisses. Michael yearned to be a part of Isabella's life, but could he let go of the past and embrace the love of a lifetime?

SDCNM1102